Then There Was You

By

Candace Shaw

Blurb

She promised herself not to give into temptation but some promises were meant to be broken.

Brooklyn Vincent is burned out from dealing with annoying bridezillas, bridal parties, and other celebratory occasions. As the head photographer of Precious Moments Events, she's ready to branch out after helping her friends achieve their dreams but has yet to fulfill her own. When the irresistible Chase Arrington reappears in her life, she decides starting a new relationship at the moment wouldn't be wise considering she's at a crossroads. However, one night together turns into more.

After a year sabbatical, Chase is ready to take over his family's Memphis law firm, but a detour to St. Simons Island has him falling for the beautiful woman he's always adored from afar. While he understands Brooklyn's fears of starting a new relationship, at the same time he knows they are meant to be ever since their eyes met. Can he convince her home is truly where the heart is?

Chapter One

"All right, you guys," Brooklyn Vincent said, focusing the camera to capture the four pre-teen cousins who were taking a break from their volleyball game on the beach. Shifting her barefeet on the warm, light brown beach sand, she peered at the screen framing them to make sure it would be the perfect picture. The girls were dressed in cute, matching, flowery sundresses over bathing suits while the boys wore T-shirts and swim trunks. "Say, 'The beach rocks!'"

"The beach rocks!" the two young ladies who were sisters repeated with bright, beautiful smiles while posing as if they were top fashion models with one hand on the hip and the other hand tousling their wet hair. The boys, however, didn't crack a smile and instead went for the suave approach—heads lifted up, hand under chins, and kneeling down in the sand.

"I see everyone has swag today," she teased, snapping more pictures as they changed poses from serious to silly.

"That's right, Ms. Brooklyn," Lana, the oldest at twelve, stated. "We slay," she said with a finger snap in a half-circle. "All day."

"Okay, you all. Back to your tournament." Brooklyn laughed as they ran back to the volleyball net to finish the girls versus boys game.

She proceeded toward the huge, white tent centered over an outdoor plank floor where her best friend, Reagan Richardson, and her family were eating barbecue, playing spades, and fellowshipping together. In a few moments Reagan's boyfriend, Dr. Blake Harrison, was going to propose. Brooklyn had been commissioned to capture the precious moment turning the barbecue—which included his family as well—into an engagement party. Without a doubt, she knew her best friend would say yes with no hesitation. Brooklyn made brief eye contact with the groom-to-be as he slammed down his card in the spades game, did a celebration dance with his partner, and proceeded to make his way to Reagan. Brooklyn knew the signal would be him clasping Reagan's hand, heading out of the tented area, and onto a romantic walk along the shore.

Brooklyn began to do a few practice shots to verify she could capture the proposal at a distance, when her friend and business partner, Addison Arrington's long, fiery red hair bounced past in the shot and she screamed in excitement, "Look who's here!"

Brooklyn pivoted with the camera—which still held her attention on its screen—to see who Addison was elated to hug only to discover it was her older brother, Chase. Brooklyn's stomach churned into a knotted twist and flames flushed her entire body despite the fact it was a breezy end-of-August day on St. Simons Island, Georgia. She snapped a picture of the siblings' embrace along with one of Chase alone and immediately turned away to suppress the heated smile which wanted to emerge as she noted his upper arm muscles peeking out from under his Yale law school T-shirt. He was intriguingly handsome as usual wearing a jaw-dropping smile across his face, which was the smooth shade of a rich, dark coffee she'd craved to sip. His bald head glistened in the sunlight, and a five o'clock shadow added an even more distinguished persona along with his glasses. Reagan had teased in the past about him being somewhat of the brainy one out of him and his fraternal twin brother, Hunter. However, Brooklyn always admired Chase's intelligent charisma the few times they'd spoken. She found his nerdy swag rather sexy.

The wind drifted his articulate tenor voice her way as he and Addison neared the tent discussing the upcoming months. Brooklyn knew Chase had been in the area for the past week, an hour away in Jacksonville, Florida preparing to teach a law class that semester at the university. She rarely saw him for he lived in Memphis, but thanks to her career as the photographer and accountant with Precious Moments Events, she would see him at weddings and other events when his family needed a photographer. The only person who knew of the silly crush was Reagan, who gave a knowing smirk before Blake grabbed her hand and whisked them toward the ocean as her white sundress blew in the wind.

Brooklyn cleared her mind of Chase and focused her attention on the couple strolling where the sand and the water met as she continued taking pictures. Standing on the edge of the tented area, she witnessed Blake kneel on one knee and her best friend's radiant face light up as tears streamed down her cheeks. Brooklyn's eyes became misty but she held back her tears while documenting with pictures of the joyous occasion. Reagan's cousin, Zaria Richardson-Braxton, stood next to Brooklyn video recording on her cell phone because they were both made of aware of Blake's intentions the day before.

"I'm so happy for her," Zaria whispered, with a sniff. "Plus, it's about damn time our girl finally stopped running from love."

Brooklyn snapped some more shots while a wave landed on the shore, knocking Reagan and Blake over as they laughed and kissed, creating the ideal picture to frame.

"He's perfect for her, Z. Like you and Garrett were meant to be no matter how much you denied it."

"I wonder who's next?" Zaria questioned before joining the rest of their family and friends in cheering and clapping as the newly engaged couple approached the tent with Reagan flashing her ring.

Thirty minutes later, after the excitement somewhat died down, Brooklyn joined a table with some of the ladies admiring the pictures of the engagement on the camera's screen. Brooklyn's concentration was strained as Chase and a few of the other men were at the next table chatting with the groom-to-be. She kept her stare downcast on the photos for if she lifted her eyes they would be on him and the tempting smile he possessed. His voice and infectious laughter were pure, sweet torture, and her mind traveled to almost eight years ago to the first time she ever heard him laughing across the room at his cousin Shelbi Arrington's wedding rehearsal. The smoothness of the sound had glided along Brooklyn's skin like a fine silk scarf and had aroused a curiousness as she'd pivoted toward the man who owned such a provoking laugh. Their eyes had met immediately and a tingling rush soared through her veins when he offered a smile so alluring she nearly fell in love at that moment. However, she'd ended her first long-term relationship the week before and pursuing another one wasn't on her list at the time. Instead, she'd admired Chase Arrington from afar over the years and always made sure to sneak a few pictures of him at events.

"Beautiful," a deep, seductive voice said behind her. "Just beautiful."

Brooklyn froze at Chase's voice and a heated sensation of ecstasy swept through every part of her body. She'd tried so hard not to glance up at him that she hadn't noticed he'd moved from his seat and now stood behind her chair. He leaned over her left shoulder to admire the engagement pictures and a whiff of his robust cologne filled her nose. She inhaled it and cleared her throat, hoping to sound as normal as possible to answer him. However, when his cheek grazed hers as he leaned even farther forward, Brooklyn simply handed him the camera considering the ladies had seen all of the pictures and left. Giving someone her camera was a big no in her book, but the urge to turn her head and kiss him charged through her, making this one time an exception to the rule.

Girl, you are acting purely nonsensical. Let's get it together, she thought.

"Yes, Reagan and Blake are such a beautiful couple," Brooklyn complimented and sighed in her head when her voice remained steady. "I'm so happy for them."

"Me too. Being with *the one* is a wonderful feeling," he said, taking the empty seat beside her. "You know what I mean?" He glanced at her with a small smirk raised up his jaw as his bare knee accidentally bumped hers.

The touch of his skin on hers, though brief, set off another round of heat to rush through her, and the thought of jumping into the ocean to cool off was forefront in Brooklyn's head. Never had a man made her feel so sensual, and desiring to experience all of his bare skin against hers.

"Mmm-hmm," she answered, wondering why he stopped swiping as his eyes lingered thoughtfully on a picture.

"This is nice." He turned the camera toward her. "Can you make me a copy?"

Taking the camera, Brooklyn saw the picture of him and Addison hugging when he'd first arrived. She sighed in relief when he didn't swipe again for the next one was of him alone, which she'd snuck in as Addison had walked ahead. Brooklyn hadn't taken the time to peek at it until now, but it seemed as though he was staring at her. Of course it was absurd, but the way the corners of his mouth inched up and the awareness of his deep gaze suggested he'd purposely turned his head to steal a glance at the same time she snapped the picture.

Brushing aside her ridiculous notion, she placed the camera next to her on the table and turned it off so he couldn't swipe to the next picture. "Of course, and I have the perfect frame for it."

"Thank you," he said, his voice filled with sincerity. "My mother would love this. She has a huge round table in the foyer filled with family pictures."

"I'll leave it with Addison." Brooklyn felt at ease with him and wondered where all the silliness of being nervous around him had arose. Yes, he was handsome, intelligent, and articulate; all the traits she loved in a man. However, she was a grown woman at thirty-two, and the crush she'd developed in her early twenties needed to be left in that decade of her life. Yet there was something about him that drove her insane whenever he was near.

"Cool. Or I may see you around. We'll be neighbors for a spell. Addi has convinced me to stay in her tiny house for the next two weeks instead of a hotel while the home the university has provided is having renovations because of the tropical storm. Honestly, I don't know how I'm going to fit in the guest loft, but I don't want to disappoint my sister even though at six foot three I'm rather concerned about bumping my head." Chuckling, he patted his shiny, bald head. "What do you think? Will I survive? I've only seen pictures of it."

Brooklyn's heart did a somersault followed by a backwards flip. The tiny house in question was parked in her backyard. While she'd been in it comfortably several times, she was sure Chase would feel cramped in the three-hundred-square-foot space, especially the guest loft which had to be accessed by using the rock climbing wall or the attached ladder.

"I'm sure it will be fine. Besides, you'll be out and about. The weather here on the island is pleasant during this time of the year. I totally doubt you'll be spending much time in the tiny house."

"Yeah, you're right. I'm looking forward to something different while I'm away from Memphis. Baby sis swears I'm a square and need loosening up. She's trying to plan a camping trip while I'm here. We'll see, but I know Ms. Adventurer isn't going to give up."

At age twenty-five, Addison was the youngest and most daring of the ladies of Precious Moments Events. She loved traveling the country visiting national parks, hiking, rock climbing, or other outdoor excursions. She'd decided a year ago to use some of her trust fund money from her parents and have a tiny home built to hitch up to her truck and hit the road.

"Yeah, I went with her once on a camping trip. It was cool … well, until the ziplining through the forest and the black bear spotting. While I did capture some awesome photos, it was still a little scary."

"She's the adventurous one out of my siblings, but I'll try almost anything once."

"You know, Addison usually joins me for dinner a few nights a week so feel free to come as well."

A surprised smile smoothed across his face as his lips parted to showcase his pearly white teeth, and her heart did the stupid flip once more. She couldn't believe her brain had even produced the suggestion; however, seeing his smile made it all the more worthwhile.

"Thank you. I'd love to, and I can help cook as well. I know you ladies have long days with Precious Moments."

And he cooks? Mmm … maybe I need to reinstate my crush.

"Addison and I would love it. We mostly order take out."

"No, you two need more than just take out." Chase hesitated for a moment as if he wanted to say something else, but instead he stood and gave a reluctant half smile as Addison motioned for him to join her at the volleyball net. "Well, it was great seeing you again and actually hold a real conversation for once unless you were avoiding me all those times." He raised a curious eyebrow as if he knew that's exactly what she was doing.

"Ha ha," Brooklyn giggled nervously, running her hands through her dark brown hair. "No, of course not. When I'm in my professional mode I tend to focus on the event. I want my clients pleased with the pictures."

"I understand. Perhaps now we can chat and," he paused, lingering his gaze on her, "finally get to know each other." Scanning around, he leaned in toward her ear. "Honestly, I wanted to ask you out the second I saw you at Shelbi's wedding, but I was informed you were in a relationship."

"Oh." Brooklyn tried to hold in the ear-to-ear grin wanting to expose itself, but it didn't happen. "Yes, I'd recently ended a relationship, and the next time I saw you at my brother's wedding to your cousin, you had a date."

"And yet I couldn't stop staring at the most beautiful woman in the room." Winking at her, Chase strolled toward the volleyball game as they were picking new teams.

Brooklyn sat numb for a moment as his words repeated over and over in her head. It had never occurred to her he even knew she existed and had wanted to ask her out. At least he'd been respectful to the fact she was in a relationship... or thought she was in one when they'd met. Of course that was eons ago, and while she was flattered with his honesty, Brooklyn decided she wasn't going to read too much into it. According to Addison, Chase was only scheduled to teach a few law classes at the university for the fall semester before beginning work at their family's law firm in the new year.

"Hey, you!"

Brooklyn shook herself out of her daze to see Reagan standing in front of her wearing a huge grin on her face. She'd changed into a pair of white shorts with a pink tank top considering her and Blake were drenched after being knocked over by the wave. Her thick, natural curly hair was piled high on her head with a hair clip. Grabbing her camera, Brooklyn snapped a few pictures so she could preserve the true happiness radiating from her best friend.

"I'm so ecstatic for you," Brooklyn said, showing her the pictures. "These are breathtaking."

"Thank you, and while I'm indeed over the moon …" Reagan paused, taking a moment to glance at her fiancé before sitting in the chair next to Brooklyn and scooting it as close as possible. "That's not why I was cheesing," she whispered. "I saw you talking to Chase."

"He was admiring your proposal photos. That's all."

"From where I was standing, it seemed like he was admiring you. I've always sensed that he likes you. You know he's staying with Addi for a bit, right? You're bound to run into him … I mean, he'll be in your backyard after all. Very convenient."

Brooklyn shrugged it off. "No big deal." *Okay, I'm lying and I'm sure Reagan knows it.*

"Now I know who to toss my bouquet to." Reagan pinched Brooklyn on her arm.

"Whatever. Let me know when you and Blake want to do your engagement photos." Brooklyn had to change the subject. "I have some ideas in mind."

"Will do. And will you do me the pleasure of being my maid of honor?"

"Of course. You're my best friend."

"Perfect. Zaria has agreed to be my matron of honor and Shelbi, Addison, and Blake's sisters as bridesmaids. I'm so excited! And don't think I didn't realize how you changed the subject."

"Whatever." Brooklyn swished her mouth to the side in a sarcastic smirk. "You have a date in mind?"

"No, but I want a late spring wedding so we'll start planning soon. Zaria has already made herself my wedding planner, and I have a book full of ideas I've been collecting since I met Blake."

"Wow, you sensed he was the one, huh?" Brooklyn asked, remembering when Reagan first met Blake on the beach while she was in a yoga class. Blake jogged by and was instantly smitten with her.

Reagan nodded her head wearing another bright smile enhancing her dimples even more. "Yes. I think when you meet the person you're going to spend the rest of your life with you just know," she answered in a whimsical sing-song voice. "And nothing can stand in the way of true love."

Those words haunted Brooklyn later on that evening as she sat in her dark room printing out the pictures of the proposal to make a book for Reagan. The picture Chase had requested was framed and staring at her on the work table. Witnessing the siblings overjoyed to see each other caused her to miss her big brother, Rasheed, and the sudden overwhelming of homesickness crept into her spirit as it had for the past year. She was at a crossroads in her life with career decisions, goals, and the dreams she'd placed on hold in order to help others facilitate theirs. However, she was ready to make a change and hoped her friends and business partners would understand.

Chapter Two

"This is nice. Um … tiny but nice," Chase commented while searching for the right words to say as he stood in the middle of the living area of Addison's home. "It definitely has character and spunk. Eclectic. Like you, Journey." He used the family's nickname for her since she was never in the same place long and loved to travel wherever on a whim. He was surprised she'd been with Precious Moments for almost two years, but still managed to travel the states by taking on event planning jobs away from St. Simons Island.

"Thank you. I know it may seem odd to some … well, everyone in our family, but for me this is all I need. You know I'm a simple girl."

"Ha! Yeah, a simple girl who's favorite hobby is to swim with the sharks." He said it sarcastically even though he was quite sure she'd done it before. Like the words "Free Spirit" printed in black across her white T-shirt read, Addison had always been a free spirit. She was simplistic, never taking herself too seriously, and didn't care about the expensive, finer things in life.

"It was fun, too. You should come next time."

"I'll pass. But seriously," he paused to peer around the three-hundred-square-foot tiny house with admiration for his sister. "I'm proud of you and your home. It fits your adventurist type of lifestyle."

"Thank you. Zoe loved it, and I can't wait until Hunter visits," Addison stated, referring to their other siblings. "Well, let's take a tour."

On one half of the longest wall, there was a small yet well-equipped kitchen with two white cabinets on either side of a picture window, baby blue antique-style appliances, and stainless steel counter tops. A small island sectioned off the area and a two-seater couch and a wicker chair finished out that side. The opposite wall had a flat screen television over a small antique wood dresser, storage shelves, the front door and stairs led to Addison's loft. Each stair opened for storage. Underneath the master loft was the bathroom with a walk-in closet, and on the opposite facing side was the guest loft above the kitchen and an area designated for an office or yoga room when the desk was hidden like a Murphy bed.

The outside of the house reminded him of a train caboose. A rock climbing wall on the backside led to a mini deck with collapsible rails on the roof, and the other half had two solar panels. It was all practical and definitely represented Addison's free spirit and on-the-go personality. Even though their family was skeptical at first, Chase could see why she decided to go this route. All she had to do was hitch it to her truck and travel to whatever adventure awaited.

Still, Chase couldn't believe he'd let his sister talk him into crashing there. He'd been staying at a hotel since he arrived two weeks ago to prepare for classes. The house the university provided had sustained damage from a storm before his arrival and was undergoing renovations they promised would be done in a week. Now it was going on two weeks and he'd grown tired of the hotel. When Addison offered, he'd immediately said yes without thinking it through. Now, as he glared with concern at the rock climbing wall leading to the guest loft, after having toured the tiny bathroom with the shower stall sure to be the death of him (or at least leave a dent in his head if he stood all the way straight), he was having second thoughts. However, he looked forward to the experience. Plus, the beautiful eye-candy a few feet away would make the stay even more pleasant.

His mind wandered to Brooklyn Vincent while his sister explained to him the best way to climb the wall by using the green rocks only. Chase had been smitten with the gorgeous photographer ever since laying eyes on her at his cousin Shelbi's wedding. That had been almost eight years ago. While he thought Brooklyn was the cutest and most adorable young lady he'd ever seen, he'd witnessed her blossom into a beautiful, confident, and sexy woman. She still had the adorable aura especially when she smiled. The beauty of it hadn't changed, and it drew his attention to her in the first place.

"So, try it out."

Addison's voice jerked Chase out of his thoughts and for a moment he assumed she was referring to trying out Brooklyn. A wicked smirk emerged as his mind flashed back to the way Brooklyn's jean shorts hugged her hips and bottom at the barbecue. His gaze had drifted onto her as she'd snapped pictures of Reagan and Blake in the distance during the proposal. All eyes were on the happy couple, but all Chase viewed was toned, supple legs and thighs that he had an urge to entangle himself with. Her skin was a smooth milk chocolate, and her tresses of dark brown waves with subtle blonde highlights fell a few inches below her shoulders. However, he knew there was so much more to her than a cute face and a banging body. She was independent and ambitious, securing her own future despite the fact her big brother, Rasheed, was an ex basketball player who was now part owner of his old NBA basketball team and worth millions. Chase had always been impressed with Brooklyn's determination to succeed on her own, which turned him on more than anything.

"Ready or are you chicken?" Addison asked while clucking sarcastically. "Or you can use the ladder, but I know you're no punk!"

Chuckling, Chase breathed in and grabbed onto the green rocks until he reached the top of the loft area with a triangle-arched ceiling. There was a full size mattress on the hardwood floor covered in a flowered quilt, a ton of colorful tossed pillows, and a nightstand with two drawers. He couldn't stand all the way up but at least he could crawl to the bed which was more comfortable than the hotel bed. There was a half a wall to block the loft for privacy. A skylight above led to the rooftop, and there were long, rectangle windows on each wall. One of the windows peered out to a wooded area beyond the fence and the other one peeked right into Brooklyn's home. He caught a glimpse of her shadow walking past the blinds in the room above the garage before a light went out.

"Whatcha think of my little space?" Addison questioned, climbing up and sitting on the edge as her feet dangled over.

"I think I may need a chiropractor after this," he said, rubbing his neck. "No, I'm kidding. It's unique. Very you."

"And mortgage free."

"You've always been practical and smart when it comes to your finances."

"I will always live well-below my means. I'd rather spend my money on traveling, seeking new adventures, and trying different cuisines. There's more besides Memphis barbecue, you know."

"You sure about that? You know you love ribs."

"I did have plenty today. Plus, Brook makes delicious barbecue, especially chicken wings. She usually does a batch for football and basketball games. You should join us sometime since you'll be here for the next few months."

"She invited me to dinner while I'm staying with you."

Addison's eyebrows rose and a devilish grin crossed her face. "Oh really? Am I invited or is this a romantic dinner?"

Surprised by her response, he decided to remain neutral. "Definitely not. She mentioned you two eat dinner together a couple of nights a week."

"Mmm-hmm. True, but … um … you know she has a crush on you."

He wrinkled his forehead and frowned. *No, it's the other way around.* "Crush? We're not in high school. Besides, Brooklyn barely speaks to me. I don't think she knows I'm alive." *Great, now I sound like a sixteen-year-old high school nerd.*

"Oh, trust me. *She knows.* We've never actually discussed it, but I overheard her and Reagan chatting about you. Plus, there's a … wait, no, I'm not going to tell you." Darting her eyes away, Addison climbed back down the rock wall and plopped on the couch, looking up at him. "My lips are sealed."

"There's a what?" Chase asked, wondering if he would be able to climb down as easily. There was a rope ladder as well, but he was scared he'd break it or his neck if he fell. "What, Addi?"

She was quiet for a moment in contemplation mode. "Fine." Addison rolled her eyes and smacked her lips at the same time. "She has a collage of pictures she's taken over the years on the wall in her home studio."

"Well, she *is* a photographer," he replied, curious to what she was alluding to.

"Brook has a picture of you at Hunter's wedding reception smack dab in the middle of the collage. You're looking away from the camera, holding a drink, your bow tie is hanging off and your tux coat is opened. One of your top buttons to your shirt is unbuttoned. I guess you could say it's quite debonair, and you weren't posing for the picture which makes it natural."

"And?" He tried to shrug it off but was surprised and rather elated that perhaps Brooklyn was more into him than he realized.

"Nothing. I wanted you to know. It's up to you what you do with the information."

*

Later on that night, Chase lay awake staring up at the stars through the skylight and thinking about his present life. He was happy with his decision to resign as the assistant district attorney at the beginning of the year to take a sabbatical before rejoining and taking over his mother's law firm. He hadn't planned on teaching pre law classes to end out his year off. However, after running into a law school buddy who was over the division and needed an adjunct professor, Chase decided to volunteer. He'd taught pre law classes at the University of Memphis in the past and had contemplated doing so again.

But there was another part of him that wasn't happy. Since Chase turned thirty-seven, he'd wrestled with the fact that his life had literally flown by and what exactly had he accomplished? Sure, he'd been one of the youngest assistant district attorneys, came from a prestigious family, and was now taking over his mother's law firm that had been in her family for generations. He felt something was missing in life as he was nearing forty. He'd always wanted a wife and children one day, but with his hectic schedule, dating had turned into a chore or an unwelcome distraction. His family said his serious side and always purposely staying busy turned women off even though he was bored with them. They simply didn't pique his interests to develop a meaningful relationship—but one woman always did during the far in-between times of being in her presence.

Yawning, he turned his head toward the window that faced Brooklyn's home and saw a light flick on. He could make out her hour glass, five foot three silhouette through the blinds. Her curves were dangerous, and he imagined running his hands along them and drawing her into him for a deep kiss on her full, pouty lips. The light went off and he closed his eyes as thoughts of her filled his sleep.

*****

"Gotta go to work, big bro. There's breakfast food in the fridge, and I made a pot of coffee. Spare keys and alarm code are on the kitchen island."

Chase heard his sister's fast-paced shout through his dreams, and the door shut which shot his eyes fully open to rest on the skylight with the sun streaming through. Groaning, he turned his head toward the clock on the nightstand which read 8:36. He remembered Addison had a brunch event to attend. Yawning, he sat up as the strong aroma of coffee perked his senses. He remade the bed as best as possible considering he couldn't stand all the way, and grabbed his cell phone and watch from the nightstand.

Twenty minutes later, he'd showered and was dressed in a pair of jeans while he waited for the iron to heat so he could press his shirt. He sipped his strong coffee while perusing the refrigerator. He wasn't an early morning eater, but his sister did remember he loved coffee upon awakening.

A movement outside of the kitchen window caught his attention, and he spotted Brooklyn clipping herbs from the potted garden on the patio. She was dressed in blue plaid pajama pants that enhanced her cute little derriere, a pink half apron, and a white tank top with her hair swept over her left shoulder. Her feet were bare, and he could make out purple nail polish. If she was going to be his breathtaking view every morning for the next week, bumping his head in the tiny house would be worth it.

Taking the few steps to the door, he opened it and stuck his head out. "Good morning," Chase greeted, standing on the little wooden front porch of the tiny house.

"Oh!" A startled gasp from Brooklyn sounded out as she raised her head. Her eyes blinked several times when they settled on his chest and then darted to his face. Running her empty hand through her hair, she cleared her throat. "Hey. You're up early."

"I'm a morning person," he stated matter-of-factly while noting her gaze wandering back to his chest.

She stood on her tippy toes and rose her head up a tad. "I see you don't have any bruises or dents," she commented with a teasing smile. "You must've managed not to bump your head on the ceiling in the guest loft."

"Barely," he said, rubbing the top of his head. "Doing some gardening?"

"No, needed some herbs to add to an omelet."

"Ahh ... are you working today, as well?" he asked, not wanting to hold her up even though he didn't want to let her go either.

"Luckily, no. Did Addi already leave for her event?"

Sipping his coffee, he nodded his head. "Yeah, about thirty minutes ago."

"See you have your coffee. Addison mentioned that's a must have for you."

"Yep, first thing in the morning," he said, taking another sip.

"Have you eaten yet?"

His eyebrow rose and his voice lowered into a deep curiosity. "Why no."

"You can join me for breakfast if you'd like."

He noted the gulp on Brooklyn's throat as if she was shocked those words uttered from her mouth.

"I'd love to," he said quickly before she changed her mind. "You need some help?"

"No ... it's almost done." A smile brightened her face. "Just bring yourself ... and a shirt," she added, glancing down at his bare abdomen.

Chuckling, Chase took another sip of his coffee. "All right. I'll finish dressing. See you in about fifteen minutes, and I'll bring the coffee."

"Perfect. I'll leave the patio door unlocked."

"Cool. So it's a date?" he purposely asked to see how she would react and respond considering the newfound information from Addison.

Her forehead wrinkled, pronouncing a cute indentation on her left cheek. She eyed him carefully while he assumed she searched her brain for an answer. Shifting her balance from one leg to the other, Brooklyn placed a hand over her brow to block the sun that had begun to peek out from behind Addison's home. Chase admired the way the natural light brushed across her skin and radiated her beautiful warm brown hue even more. Thoughts of running his hands over the silkiness of her filled his head, and he was relieved she began to speak before he reached out to act upon his daydream.

"Noooooooo …" She brushed her hand through her hair again and a released a cute giggle. "Just breakfast."

"I was teasing. Trust me. Our first date won't be at your house."

"Oh, is that right?" Leaning against the door, she folded her arms over her chest. "Our first date?"

"Yes, most definitely. I think it's safe to say we both know it's bound to happen. See you soon." Winking, he turned on his heel and went inside the house before Brooklyn could say anything else.

His admiration for Brooklyn had been there since the moment he met her, and now he believed staying at his sister's home wasn't by chance but was fate.

Chapter Three

Did I really invite him to breakfast? Alone? Brooklyn questioned herself as she slid the pan of a dozen homemade biscuits out of the oven. Placing them on the stove next to the skillet with the herb and country ham omelet, she untied her apron and shoved it into a nearby drawer. It was bad enough she couldn't shake Chase's glorious chocolate-coated body out of her head. When he'd said good morning and startled her, her gaze landed on his abs that she could scrub her clothes on if her washing machine ever gave out. Once she finally jerked her stare to his face, she was surprised to see him without his glasses. She found him handsome and distinguished— and even nerdy in a cute way—with them on. However, without he was a tad more charming ... or it could be the shirtless image she couldn't yank from her thoughts.

A light tap, followed by the chime of the alarm indicating the backdoor was opening, turned her head in the direction. Brooklyn's heartbeat sped up, but she reminded herself to stay calm and remember the silly crush she once had for Chase had ended and his ridiculous date suggestion wasn't going to happen.

Chase strolled through the mudroom leading to the eat-in-kitchen where moments before she'd hurriedly set the table with the guest china, juice glasses, silverware on white cloth napkins, and coffee cups. How she managed to do so within a fifteen minute span along with finishing the omelet, brushing her teeth, and washing her face with thirty seconds to spare that allowed her to remember to breathe correctly in his presence was beyond impossible.

He carried the stainless steel carafe of coffee in one hand and creamer in the other. Brooklyn was relieved he wore a Yale Law school sweatshirt, but it did nothing to hide the fact she knew the scrumptious Adonis chest and muscular biceps that laid underneath it.

"Hey, you're just in time," she said, placing the biscuits onto a white, oval platter. "Everything is done." She motioned for him to sit at the kitchen table as he placed his items in the middle and surveyed the table scene.

"This is rather nice for an impromptu invite." He walked over to her chair and pulled it out for her before sitting down in his. "Is your table always set?"

"Uh ... no. It's usually filled with magazines, photos, and junk mail." She laughed sarcastically because she'd stuffed all of it into the kitchen junk drawer after she invited him to breakfast. "Well, dig in." Brooklyn handed him the serving spoon for the grits.

"No, ladies first." He spooned out some grits onto her plate. The cheddar cheese oozed through. "Mmm ...cheese grits. My fav."

Once their plates were full, they ate in silence for a few moments as he complimented her on everything.

"These biscuits are delicious," he stated, spreading strawberry marmalade on one of the halves. "I love homemade biscuits. Reminds me of growing up."

"Thank you. My mother's recipe. I make them on Sundays like she used to before she got sick."

He nodded empathetically with wistful eyes as if he knew her mother had lost her battle with breast cancer and her father had died a year later from a heart attack. Brooklyn was a senior in high school upon her father's death, and Rasheed, who was a starting point guard in the NBA at the time, was appointed her legal guardian until she turned eighteen.

"Are you ready for your first day of classes?" she asked, needing to change the subject before she became teary eyed. It had been years since losing her parents, but a day never went by that she didn't miss them.

"Yes. I sent out the syllabus and met with a few of the students already."

"I know this is only temporary, but why did you decide to make this part of your year off? Addi said you were having fun traveling Europe and Africa."

Taking the last bite of his omelet, he answered when he was finished chewing. "When I was the assistant DA, I taught pre law at University of Memphis a few nights a week. I enjoyed it, but my day job became demanding, and I had to let it go. My law school friend is over the division at UNF. He mentioned he needed an adjunct professor for the semester while one of his professors is out on maternity leave. I volunteered as a joke, and he took me seriously. And well, here I am." He shrugged with a light laugh. "Professor Arrington."

"Has a nice ring to it, but you aren't staying for a second semester? Right?" A tiny jab pierced her heart when she asked the question, as if it had finally occurred to her that his stay in the Georgia/Florida area was temporary.

"No, the other professor will be back. Plus, I made a promise to my mother years ago to take over her family's law firm when she retired. I worked there for a couple of years after law school before leaving. She was happy for me, but I know deep down she wanted all four of us to run the firm how my cousins are all doctors and own my Uncle Frances and Aunt Darla's medical practice." He paused, taking the last swig of his orange juice. "The law firm has been in my mom's family for three generations. Zoe passed the bar earlier this year and now works there full-time. My twin decided to go in a different direction with Doctors Unlimited, and well ... Addison... you know she has no interest much to my mother's chagrin."

"No, but who knows, perhaps one day Addi will," Brooklyn said in a hopeful tone, but she knew that wasn't going to happen.

"Well, she loved to debate with the family growing up. For the youngest she definitely wanted to prove us all wrong and present enough evidence and exhibits to prove her case. Of course the Judge adores his baby girl so she always won in our father's eyes. So, yes, one day if she ever decides to go to law school. She passed the LSAT but shocked us all when she decided to move here and work with Precious Moments Events. Of course all she did in college was plan events so I'm not surprised."

"Well, we're happy to have Addison here even if it's only temporary."

"Addi has always been fly-by-the-seat of her pants. She's our little Journey. Wherever the wind blows, so does she along with her tiny house and truck. What about you? What made you decide to move to St. Simons?"

"I needed a change. I'd been in Memphis for most of my life except for college, but I moved back home after graduation. I needed a new experience. I'm an accountant as far as my degrees and career, but photography had always been a hobby of mine since middle school. However, when I returned to Memphis something was missing, and it no longer felt like home to me. When the opportunity presented itself, I moved here to assist Reagan with her dream—" She abruptly stopped, deciding not to tell him that deep down she was ready for a change again.

Brooklyn enjoyed her career, but she no longer wanted to deal with bridezillas and their attitudes. She still wanted to be a photographer but not in an event type of setting and had begun to delve more into creative photography.

Thoughts of owning a photography studio to teach and mentor budding photographers had also crossed her mind, and she figured she could do both.

"Yes, I remember when you turned your hobby into a side-career. That's kinda how we met. You were always at events snapping pictures and avoiding me whenever I wanted to chat."

She stuffed the last of her omelet into her mouth and chewed slowly as he stared at her knowingly.

Dabbing her lips with a napkin, she glanced away and then settled her eyes directly on his. "I wasn't avoiding you. I was at work. I didn't have time to make small talk."

"So I should've hired you to get your attention?"

"Or asked me out." *Wait, did I say that? Out loud?* Her eyes grew wide as he leaned in with a serious expression as if he was going to do so.

"Does that offer still stand?"

"I was joking, like you were earlier." Laughing it off, Brooklyn fidgeted with her fingers under the table.

"No, you're not joking and neither am I."

"That was eons ago, and we wouldn't work out now anyway."

A curious grin slid up his left jaw as he sat back in his chair. "Why do you think that?"

"You're only here for the semester and then back to our hometown."

"Scared you're going to fall in love with me while I'm here?"

She smacked her lips together. "Boy, please." Standing, she grabbed their empty plates with the silverware and headed to the sink so he wouldn't notice her flushed face.

Chase collected the mugs and juice glasses. "Boy? I'm a grown man ... which you witnessed earlier." Setting the dishes in the soapy, hot water, he took the dish cloth from her. "You cooked. I'll wash the dishes."

Placing her back against the counter next to him, she folded her arms across her chest as the memory of his

Godiva-kissed abs and muscular biceps popped in her head once more. "Please, no one was paying attention to you. I've seen half naked men before. For example, last week, all the groomsmen in an upcoming wedding were shirtless on the beach for their photo shoot. Trust me, they all had six packs and I wasn't salivating over any of them."

"They weren't me," he whispered in her ear as an arrogant smirk etched his face. "I'm sure I saw you bite your bottom lip."

You got that right, she thought.

"Whatever." She shrugged, taking a plate from him and drying it before placing it in the cabinet.

"I need your expertise on something," he started.

"Finances or photography?"

"That's right, you're a double-threat … or actually triple-threat. You could add Chef Vincent to your resume. Breakfast was delicious. But seriously, I have to turn in a picture to the university to go along with my bio that's already on the website. The deadline is in a couple of days. I have some photos in my cellphone that I took." Chase dried his soapy hands on the dish towel and slid his phone from the case on his slacks. "Can you help me select one?" He pulled the pictures up and handed her the phone.

"Of course." She scrolled through the headshots he'd obviously taken with a selfie-stick. While he was drop-dead handsome in every single one of them, none of them would work.

"Chase, your pictures are nice, but they're clearly selfies and the resolution isn't high enough for a website. You need professional pictures. I can do them for you."

"Thank you. I appreciate it."

"What are you doing this afternoon?"she asked, setting his phone on the counter.

"I have a law school mixer on campus to attend followed by a dinner party at the president's home this evening for faculty to toast off the new school year." He glanced at the clock on the microwave. "In fact, I need to leave soon. What about tomorrow afternoon? I only have two morning classes. I can be back over here by two."

"Meet me here at three. It shouldn't take long and you can meet your deadline."

"Cool." He glanced at the clock again and a reluctant sigh escaped him. "I hate to eat and run, but I need to change for the mixer."

"No problem," she began as she walked him toward the patio door. "You have over an hour drive to Jacksonville. I suggest you leave extra early in the morning. The interstate will be backed up during the morning rush hour. Quite a few people live on the island but work in Brunswick and Jacksonville. I guess you'll be relieved when your rental home by campus is ready." The thought of it made her heart contract for some reason, and it must have shown on her face for he tilted his head to the side with a curious scrunch of his nose.

"Yeah, but this gives me a chance to hang with Addi. And …" he paused, stepping into her personal space, "hopefully to learn more about you, as well. Something I've wanted to do for a long while."

His voice lowered at the last part of his comment, and a lump lodged in her throat as his intense stare suggested he could read her thoughts.

"Yes, on a platonic level." Brooklyn stated it in a teasing way even though deep down she would love to learn more about him.

Chase caught her in his arms as a startled cry erupted from her throat. He lowered his lips to hers but didn't kiss her even as Brooklyn's mouth parted, and her eyes were nearly shut with anticipation. She'd imagined them in this situation a thousand times and now it was a reality.

"Don't worry. I'm not going to kiss you … yet. But I do believe in life happening naturally, and it's quite obvious there's something between us." Letting her go, he pivoted toward the door and opened it. "Can't wait to see what it is even if it's platonic, like you say, but I doubt it. We've always had an attraction to each other. You can't deny it, and now since the opportunity has presented itself, I'm going to take advantage of it." Winking, he left, shutting the door.

After locking the door, Brooklyn rested against it to settle her unraveled breathing. She'd wanted nothing more than for Chase to kiss her into a state of passionate oblivion. She craved his lips on hers for the past eight years, and the thought that the occasion had been a mere half inch away, caused her to curse out loud as she strode back to the kitchen and finished putting away the dishes. His cologne lingered in the atmosphere, and she let out an aggravated moan as she realized it had been imbedded on her skin when he held her to him.

Twenty minutes later, Brooklyn strolled into her in-home photography studio/dark room which was above the three-car garage. She had two wedding albums to finish even though her thoughts continued to roam to Chase and the almost kiss which still sent warm tingles over her body at the mere memory. Heck, he didn't even kiss her, and she couldn't control her emotions or the urge to sprint over to the tiny house to put out the fire that burned deep for him.

Settling at her work table that was scattered with 8x10 wedding photos, she tried to shake her head free of Chase so she could concentrate on creating the first album. Music always got her mind off whatever was on it, and she turned on the music app on her cell phone. She settled on the Janet Jackson station and was jamming to her greatest hits until it came to the song "If" which sent Brooklyn right back to the dilemma of her desire to be with Chase. Turning the song off after the chorus which pretty much described what she wanted to do with him, she opted for a station with instrumental music only.

Ten minutes into deciding which cake cutting photo to use, she heard the alarm of Chase's car from the driveway below, and she skirted to the window to peep through the shut blinds. He was impeccably dressed in gray slacks, a light blue dress shirt, and an argyle blue and gray sweater vest. A gray newsboy cap topped off the assemble, and she could imagine how tantalizing he smelled.

Brooklyn retreated to the task at hand with a slight smile on her face. There had been an instant attraction from the moment they'd laid eyes on each other years ago. However, it sure as hell wasn't platonic and apparently he felt the same as her. Why on earth was she so scared all of a sudden?

She'd known of him for the last eight years, though she didn't *know* him. Sure, she'd heard he was a great guy and whatnot, but that was from family and friends. Of course they'd think that. However, now she was witnessing firsthand the man she'd admired over the years was indeed a great guy. Almost too good to be true, but she couldn't become attached to him. She had to keep him at bay; however, it didn't mean she couldn't have fun with harmless flirting. As long as it didn't go any further or she'd find herself wanting more and missing Chase when he returned to their hometown.

Moments later the doorbell to the front door whisked her out of her thoughts. Jetting downstairs to answer it, she peeked out the peep hole considering she wasn't expecting company. Her heart did a triple somersault when she saw Chase on the other side.

Had he been regretting the fact that they hadn't kissed as well and was here to do so?

Opening it, she stared up at the man who wore the same intense expression when they said their good-byes earlier. Gripping the doorknob to steady her balance, Brooklyn halted the desire to say eff it and kiss him her damn self. However, his penetrating stare seeped into her being and the notion of him coming back to finish what they'd almost started bolted an electrical current to rush so hard through her it nearly knocked her off kilter. Her breathing was beginning to unravel as her mind sent her on a trip to the wicked, wild thoughts as it always did when he was near. The difference from any other time was now she had to restrain herself from actually acting upon it. Motioning for him to come in, she closed the door behind them as their eyes never left each other's face.

"Um … I-I th-thought you were heading to the um … mixer," Brooklyn managed to stammer out.

He leaned against the door with a dazed expression as if he was comprehending what she'd said. "Oh … uh … I am, but I …"

Chase's voice trailed off as his eyes widened when Brooklyn stood on her tippy toes, yanked him by the collar to her, and crushed her lips on his. The urge to kiss him had swept over her the instant he arrived, and she could no longer hold in the burning need to experience his lips ravishing hers. For a quick second, she regretted the hasty, not-like-her forward decision and was aiming to halt their ardent kiss—then she would be bound to be embarrassed to even glance at him for the rest of his stay at Addison's. However, when he hoisted her up until her legs encircled tight around his waist and turned them so her back was against the door, she no longer regretted her decision. Chase became in control of their kiss as if he'd made the first move. He delved deeper into her mouth, swirling his tongue with hers as relieved sounds escaped them both.

Brooklyn opened her eyes for a second and nearly laughed when she noticed his glasses were fogged up.

"Uh … your glasses."

"I hadn't noticed." He tossed them on the couch in the sitting room. "That's never happened. Now, where were we?" he asked, meshing her completely on him.

"You were driving me crazy."

"Let me continue," he said with a cocky snicker and imprisoned her lips once more.

All of the pent-up desire to be exactly where she was at the moment was indeed worth the wait. Her silly crush wasn't in vain after all, as the pleasure of finally experiencing the dreams while asleep and even awake were now a reality and she wasn't disappointed. His mouth and energy had taken possession. Brooklyn found herself sinking deeper into the whirlwind of passion that he bestowed upon her. No man had ever awakened her senses this much, and the crush she'd sprinted far away from transformed into something else. No, not love— even she knew that was too soon—but it wasn't lust either. It was more of a newfound awareness of the feelings she'd tried to ignore over the years whenever his name was mentioned.

Chase wove a hand into her tresses while his other one remained tight around waist. His moans turned her on even more, causing her to explore more of him, but she had to show some type of restraints. Removing her lips from his reluctantly, they stared at each other in silence except for the in-sync pounding of their hearts.

"Wow," he whispered, setting Brooklyn back on her feet but still keeping her in a tight, intimate embrace. "I wasn't expecting that at all, but I'm glad you're a woman not scared to make the first move. I was trying my hardest not to kiss you earlier, and the cold shower as soon as I left here did nothing to calm me down."

"I know," she whispered, glancing down at his pants with a slight gulp.

"You weren't supposed to know that," he stated through a clenched smirk.

"It's kind of obvious, but I'll take it as a compliment."

A ringing startled them both as their heads turned toward the kitchen. Frowning, Brooklyn tried to remember who she'd assigned the unfamiliar ringtone.

"That's my cell phone," Chase said. "That's why I'm here. I realized I'd left it when I was in the car."

"Oh," she chuckled, sliding out of his arms in embarrassment.

"I'll go retrieve it." Wearing a half grin, he trekked to the kitchen.

"Right." She nervously ran her hands through her hair, which was somewhat tangled from Chase's fingers rummaging through it. Now she was mortified for assuming he was back to finish what they'd started earlier not to retrieve his cellphone. Had she jumped too soon? She honestly didn't feel that way, but at the same time where could a relationship with him go? He lived in Memphis, and she had no intentions on moving back home.

"Got it," he said, sliding the phone into his pants.

"Okay. Um ... sooooo ..." She was back to the awkward stammering and not sure why. She didn't feel as if she'd made a mistake, but at the same time perhaps it was too soon. "You have your mixer thingy."

"I do, but should we talk?" he asked, crunching his forehead and stepping toward her.

"It was a great kiss, and we haven't even been on a date yet."

"True, but considering you don't live here perhaps going on a date would be out of the question."

A mischievous grin spread across his face. "So are you saying skip the dating part and have fun with each other? Like friends with benefits?"

"No. I'm a grown woman. I don't play those kinds of games with my heart. I'm saying let's take it slow and ..."

"Forget about the kiss right now and continue getting to know each other?"

Geez, this reading my thoughts is kinda creepy. "Something like that, but I don't regret what happened," she replied sincerely.

"Neither do I," he stated, kissing her tenderly on the forehead. "That's for the agreement."

"No problem," she replied, opening the door before she changed her mind.

"I'm glad I forgot my phone."

"Me too." She paused, not wanting him to leave. "Drive safe."

"I will," Chase answered, his eyes lingering on her face. He ran a caressing finger down her cheek before turning on his heel and heading to his car.

After he left, Brooklyn raced back to her studio and plopped down in the chair at the work table. Her eyes were immediately drawn to Chase's picture in the middle of her photo collage. For years she'd fantasized about her dream man in general, and it always ended with her thoughts on Chase. She could now add mind-blowing kisser and strong enough to hold her up to the list. She looked forward to finally learning about the man in the picture after all this time, but her heart cringed at the fact that in a few months, he would be back in Memphis.

And she missed him already.

Chapter Four

"Wow. These are fascinating pieces," Brooklyn commented as her eyes scanned over Kameryn Monroe's latest glass art collection which was being featured at Now That's Art Gallery in downtown Brunswick. "Thank you so much for inviting me for a private showing."

"Anytime. Besides, I want you to photograph them for my interview with *Art Gazette Magazine*. I know they have their own photographer, but mine is better." Kameryn winked as they continued to stroll the marble floor of the mezzanine level of the gallery used for special collections.

"I appreciate it. These glass art animals are gorgeous. I'm still intrigued at the process you and your team undertake. Heck, I could barely make the balloon animals for my nephew's birthday party." Brooklyn studied a glass cheetah hanging from the ceiling with support cables. His piercing green eyes and attack position were almost too real, causing a shiver to run down her back. "They're so life-like."

"They're all the same exact size as the real thing. I wanted them to be as authentic as possible, so my team and I did a plethora of research on how the animals move, their habitats, personalities, etc. We went on a safari tour in Africa to witness the animals up close and personal ... well, from a safe distance of course. It was a thrilling experience. It's a part of a documentary we shot that will be on repeat when the exhibit opens."

"You never cease to amaze me."

"Thank you." Lifting her braids up, Kameryn secured them in a ponytail with the scrunchie from her wrist. "I can't wait until next week's public viewing even though I'm freaking out."

Brooklyn lightly chuckled for it was the fourth time Kameryn had taken down her hair in the past ten minutes. Her nerves were indeed showing. "Girl, why? Your work is known all over the world for the past decade. You got this, my friend."

"I know, but I have jitters before any new collection."

"That's to be expected, but trust me, everyone is going to love these," Brooklyn stated, eyeing two baby elephants with their trunks hooked into a heart. "I can't wait for tomorrow's shoot."

"Me either. The other reason I invited you here is because I have a business proposition for you."

"Another one?"

"Yes. I've decided to do a book with my glass art creations. My manager thinks it's a great idea and I agree. I would love for you to be the principal photographer for the upcoming collections."

"Oh, wow. When do you need me to start?" Brooklyn asked, racking her brain of what she already had on her schedule for the rest of the year.

"Well, the Animals of Africa and Animals of the Rainforest collections will be featured in museums and botanical gardens for the next year as well as some other collections starting soon that be will scattered around in various places. Some of them I will attend the preview or private showings, so I'd definitely want you at those with me if possible. I'll provide travel and lodging so you don't have to worry, and of course I'll pay you nicely. I'm hoping you could perhaps weave it into your schedule throughout the year. I know you have your duties at Precious Moments, and I understand that comes first so I'm willing to work around your schedule because I want you to say yes. At the most, you'd probably be gone for a few days out of the month. I'd need everything complete by the summer for a November release according to the publisher. You don't have to let me know now. Think about it, but please say yes."

Brooklyn let the words soak in, realizing this was the type of opportunity she'd been searching for. She'd grown tired of photographing weddings and other events, but always looked forward to photographing outside of the box. Helping to create a book of Kameryn's glass art creations was a start in the direction she wanted to veer toward in her career.

"My schedule is somewhat lax with Precious Moments right now because it's not wedding season so that won't be an issue. And I don't need to think about it. I'd love to photograph the book for you."

Kameryn clapped. "Perfect. I'll have my assistant contact you so you two can set up a travel schedule, and she has some of the dates for the showings starting after Christmas. My manager is working on a contract for you as we speak."

Brooklyn cracked a smile. "So you knew I would say yes?"

"As a matter of fact I did ... or at least prayed you would. The last few times we've spoken, you expressed needing a change. And here it is. When the idea was brought to me for the book, you were the first person I thought of. Besides, you've shot photos of my in-the-making documentaries and they're exquisite. I want to include some of those as well."

"Thank you, but that's because of your creations. I honestly can't believe this is happening."

"No problem, Brooklyn. That's what friends are for. I'll have my assistant send you the contract. If there's something you need to change or aren't sure about, feel free to let me or her know. I want my photographer happy."

"Well, I'm happy with even being considered. I know you work with quite a few photographers."

"True, but I think this would be ideal for you. Oh, and you'll be ecstatic to know one of the places I would like to do a shoot is the Botanical Gardens in Memphis. I have a glass art flower collection that has been there since this spring, but it's being donated to a cancer treatment center in the next few months."

"Well, you know I love anything Memphis."

"You can visit your family at the same time." Kameryn glanced in her assistant's direction who'd tapped her watch. "I hate to run, but I have a fitting for tomorrow's interview. I'll text you pictures of the outfit choices so you'll know in advance even though I'd be happy in jeans and a T-shirt," she said, glancing down at her current attire. "I hope you enjoy viewing the rest of the collection."

"I'm sure I will." The ladies hugged before Kameryn scurried off with her assistant down the spiral stairs of the museum.

For the next few minutes, Brooklyn toured the glass art animals in amazement while taking note of the angles and lighting of the museum to verify if she needed to bring in more lights for certain areas. Of course Kameryn would be in some of the shots, and Brooklyn knew her casual yet chic style would blend nicely with the collection.

Later on that afternoon, Brooklyn perused the pictures of the outfit selections for tomorrow's interview and museum shoot. She wasn't surprised at the chambray flowy dress, the sleeveless leopard-print dress that would showcase Kameryn's toned arms from years of glassblowing, and ripped black jeans with a T-shirt and a pink blazer to top it off.

A tap at the door of her studio jerked her head from the pictures and onto the handsome face of Chase Arrington who leaned casually on the door jam. He wore a crisp pair of jeans, a tweed, blue sports jacket, and a gray scarf wrapped around his neck. She'd called him moments before to inform him the backdoor was unlocked and to meet her upstairs in the studio when he was ready.

"Hey there, my friend." He said it with a knowing gleam in his eyes.

Trying to keep her voice steady and her eyes from roaming over his fine physique, Brooklyn pretended to play with her camera which was already set for the shoot. She had to remind herself she couldn't jump him like she wanted to and kiss him until it drove them both insane. "You're in time for your photo session, *my friend*," she said in the same manner as him.

Sliding the scarf from around his neck, Chase slung it over the chair next to the door and continued to stroll into the room.

"Catching a cold?" she asked, nodding toward the scarf.

"Addi said it went with my outfit and slid it around my neck this morning stating I needed to be dapper for my first day."

"How was your day, *Professor* Arrington?"

"It was good overall. My first class started at eight so they were half asleep but they woke up when I mentioned the timed pop quiz."

"Geez, already?" she asked with a slight wrinkle of her nose.

"Just wanted to see what they know. It's their first law class. The grade won't count, but they'll have the same exact quiz again at the end of the semester."

"I do not miss pop quizzes or early morning classes. I tried to schedule all of my classes after nine and never on a Friday."

"Makes sense. Three day weekend."

"You know what?" She tapped her chin, glancing at the scarf. "We could use the scarf."

His eyebrows rose into a wicked pause and a sinful smile graced his face. "Oh really?" Chase approached her workstation table where she stood on the opposite side and leaned over it toward her until his lips were seconds from hers. "What did you have in mind?" he asked in a low, seductive voice.

Everything that I tossed and turned over last night. "Nothing in the gutter, that's for sure." *Okay, I'm lying.* "I meant we could snap a few pictures with it on. Gives you a charismatic look."

"Too bad because that's not what I was thinking."

Ignoring his statement as her cheeks filled with heat of possibly being tied up, Brooklyn swiped her camera and motioned for Chase to follow her to the gray backdrop. "Have a seat on the stool and we'll begin." She placed the camera on the tripod and turned to find out why he'd stopped.

"I see you have a photo collage." He strolled over to the wall and immediately pointed to the picture from his twin brother's wedding. "With my picture in the middle. Nice to be the focal point."

Brooklyn silently chastised herself for forgetting to remove it or at least move it to another spot. "Don't flatter yourself. Your picture isn't there on purpose. That's where it ended up."

Chase flashed a sarcastic smirk and proceeded to sit on the stool as Brooklyn snapped the picture. "If you say so, but I know otherwise, and I am flattered."

She turned the camera around to show him the photo. "Perfect. We're done. You can leave now," she stated sarcastically. "I'll send you the bill."

"My eyes are closed."

"I can photoshop them on," she teased. If they continued with the flirting she was sure enough going to end up with her lips right back on his.

"All right, I'll stop. Let's get serious." Chase placed his hand under his chin, then on his lap. "What position do you want me in?"

A sinful smirk spread across his face, and what was left of Brooklyn's willpower continued to fizzle away.

She glanced at the picture on the camera screen and realized the indoor background wouldn't work for the vision in her head. It may be a bio photo for a college website, but she wanted it to have some pizzazz. Plus, being in close proximity with him and the subtle innuendos were wreaking havoc on her concentration. "You know what? It's a lovely day on the island, and I think a picture with an outdoor background would be better."

Walking to her workstation, she slipped the camera in its bag and grabbed her olive green blazer from the back of the chair. After slinging the bag and the jacket over her shoulder, she headed to the door. Turning toward Chase, who wore a curious grin etched on his face, she opened the door. "Let's jet out of here. We'll take my golf cart to the Village Pier. We can take pics by the water and the brick background of the lighthouse would be nice. I've done some wedding photos there."

"Sounds good to me," he said, joining her at the door. "You don't trust yourself, huh?"

"Nope," she answered honestly.

"Me either."

"Don't forget the scarf." She winked, tossing it to him.

"And yet we keep flirting with each other. I don't think where we are matters, but I do agree with the change of scenery for the picture."

"I guess we'll go with your 'what happens will happen naturally'."

"I believe it already is."

*****

"That's right. Show me what you're working with," Brooklyn sang in a joking manner while Chase switched poses under the lighthouse in the Village Pier. "You're a natural. The camera loves you."

"Nah, I think that's you," Chase answered, winking and chuckling as she shook her head in the negative.

"In your dreams," she quipped, snapping a few more shots.

"You've been there. You don't remember?"

"Boy, bye," she answered, smacking her lips and clicking another picture.

Brooklyn had indeed been a woman he'd always admired from a far, but now that he was finally getting to know her, Chase was kicking himself for not asking her out eons ago when she lived in Memphis. Though at the time he was younger, and the thought of a serious relationship wasn't something he wanted as he focused on his career. He knew he shouldn't become attached to her because he would be returning home at the end of the year. However, he couldn't help it, and now that he'd finally had a chance to kiss her, he wanted nothing more for the opportunity to do so again and again. He did agree with taking it slow considering it could be a case of infatuation; however, the way her eyes brightened when she stared at him lit up his heart in a way it never had.

Chase had stayed up half the night imagining her warm lips kissing him with the same vigor she'd bestowed upon him in real life. Kissing her luscious lips and hearing her beautiful moans of ecstasy on his mouth stirred an ardent emotion in his spirit he couldn't shake. He was pleasantly surprised when she grabbed him by the collar and placed the unexpected, sensual kiss on him before he could do so. While he'd returned for his cell phone, when she opened the door and stared up at him with hazy eyes, his first thought was to snatch her to him and sample her pouty lips.

"Tilt your head up a bit."

Chase snapped out of his daze of staring at her lips, and followed the instructions ... or so he thought, but her face scrunched into a frown.

"No, place your chin down a tad and look at me."

"Like this?" he asked, placing his chin down and staring straight ahead.

Brooklyn strode to him and placed her hand gently on his jaw. She was in his personal space and her subtle touch along with her sweet scent aroused him. The way she turned his head slightly toward her, Chase thought for sure she was going to ravage him again with her succulent lips which were perfectly parted in a kissable pout. He certainly wouldn't hold back even though the area was full of people walking the sidewalk along the water. He wasn't sure how much longer he could hold in the restraint he'd promised himself. Brooklyn was the kind of woman he would want a long term, possibly more relationship with. However, he knew she was happy with her life and career on the little Georgia island.

"Just like that, and give me a smize."

"A smize?" he questioned, wrinkling his forehead. "That's a word?"

"Yes. It means smile with your eyes. Tyra Banks coined it on *America's Next Top Model.*"

"Ah ... I see." Pausing, he eyed her thoughtfully while his mind captured them in an intimate position. "Okay, so am I smizing?"

"Perfect," she whispered, drifting her eyes over his face while a provoking smile of her own emerged as if she had a hunch of what he was thinking. "Stay posed like that." She slid her hand away from his jaw and straightened the scarf before returning to the camera resting on the tripod.

Chase watched as Brooklyn snapped a few more pictures. He wanted like hell to know what was going on in that beautiful mind of hers. There had been a twinkle in her eye when she positioned him for the pictures, but now it was replaced with a seriousness she hadn't displayed during their fun, lighthearted photo session.

"All right. I think we're done," she said, removing the camera from the tripod. "I like the lighthouse photos the best, but the ones where you were seated on the bench with the Atlantic Ocean as a background are nice as well."

"Cool. I'll let you select the picture for my bio. I trust your expertise."

Brooklyn nodded quietly, sliding the tripod into its bag and hoisting it over her shoulders. He sensed something was bothering her all of a sudden, and he didn't know what had happened. They'd been having fun with teasing and flirting with each other. Stepping in her direction, he slid the bag from her shoulder and placed it on his. He hoped like hell she didn't regret the kiss.

"What's wrong?"

She shrugged. "Nothing," she answered with a light smile.

"You're lying."

"Yep."

"Well at least you're being honest."

"Something occurred to me. That's all."

They headed in silence back to the golf cart. He placed her belongings in the storage bin and locked it. "You want to talk about it over dinner? My treat."

"Yes, to dinner. No, to what it was. It's no biggie."

"Does it have something to do with me? Us?"

"Nothing to do with you, and there's no us, but you are a welcomed distraction from my thoughts lately."

His years of being an attorney gifted him with the knowledge of knowing when someone was being honest or not with him. He sensed her sincerity as her eyes had brightened for a second at the mention of "us."

"You have man issues? Broken heart? Something like that?"

She giggled. "No. I don't have trust or man issues. No one's ever broken my heart except when my parents died. It has nothing to do with a man."

"All right. I won't press the issue." He glanced around at all of the shops and restaurants in the Village Pier. "You have a suggestion for a restaurant?"

"Do you like burgers?" She nodded her head at the restaurant across the street from the park. "Brogen's has the best."

"Sounds good," he said, gripping her hand in his with a reassuring squeeze. "Lead the way."

Brooklyn glanced down at their hand holding while a pursed smile formed on her lips. She stared up at him with a special gleam in her eyes, shaking him to the core.

"Let's go," she said, swinging their hands together.

Chapter Five

Brooklyn hated to admit she was somewhat disappointed the short walk to Brogen's had ended and she had to let go of Chase's hand when he opened the door to the restaurant and let her pass in front of him. His hand was warm and familiar on her skin thanks to her haste to kiss him. She was glad they could be normal around each other and carry on as if there wasn't an elephant between them. But maybe she was over thinking it. Perhaps there wasn't an elephant and only she was second guessing their relationship.

They followed the hostess to an upstairs outdoor balcony booth overlooking the park, and settled into their seats.

"What's good to eat here?" he questioned, peering at her over his glasses before retreating back to his focus to the menu.

"Everything. I usually order the bacon bleu cheeseburger with the works and the zucchini fries."

"Sounds good. I'll have the same, and the potato skins for an appetizer."

"Oh, wow. We think alike. I was contemplating ordering those. They're delish with sour cream."

"Best way to eat them."

Once the waitress jotted down their order, Brooklyn took her camera out and began glancing over Chase's headshots. "These are good. It's hard to choose which one you should use."

Chase slid from his side of the booth and over to hers in a flash. "Wow. That's me?"

"Yes, it is. You're quite photogenic."

"Thanks, but I also think the photographer had something to do with it as well. You made sure I was posing and smiling ... I mean smizing correctly. Very hands on."

"Thank you." She paused as his knee brushed hers and then leaned against it. She wasn't sure if it was on purpose or the fact she was in the middle of the seat and hadn't scooted over. Nor did she want to because the hard muscle of his thigh resting on hers was warm and comforting like when he'd held her hand on the walk over. Every touch or look from him was familiar and inviting.

Her cellphone vibrating in her purse tore her from her mind beginning to wander in amorous territory, and she reached over to retrieve it. A text message from Kameryn's assistant stating to check her email had Brooklyn doing so. Her contract for the book was attached and she was dying to open it. Instead, she tossed the phone back in her purse and placed her focus on Chase's pictures.

"Everything all right?"

"Yeah," she answered, nodding reassuringly even though her heartbeat sped up. "It's some business stuff."

"Of course." Chase moved back to his side of the booth and took a sip of his water. "I guess Precious Moments Events is 24/7."

"It can be, but this isn't Precious Moments business." Brooklyn paused, realizing she wanted to tell him about the opportunity with Kameryn even though she hadn't disclosed the information to her business partners yet.

"That's right. You do freelance photography as well."

"Yes, but ..."

"What's wrong? You're wearing that same intense, deep in thought expression from earlier."

"I am?" Her face scrunched in confusion.

"Yes."

"I've had a lot on my mind lately ... career wise," she added in when she noted his eyebrow raise as if she meant him.

"I see. Trust me, I know all about career changes."

"Are you happy with your decision?"

"I am. I was stressed as the assistant DA. It's a career I thought I wanted when I initially left the firm years ago. I'd planned on following in my dad's footsteps and become a federal judge eventually. Sometimes the grass isn't always greener on the other side."

"True. Or sometimes you think someone else's dream is yours when actually it's not."

"That's what I learned. Care to explain yours?"

She hesitated, but remembered men are good with secrets. "You can't tell anyone ... well, your sister sort of knows."

"Your secret is safe with me."

"I no longer enjoy working with the event company. I'm tired of dealing with bridezillas, bridal parties, and whatnot. The only reason why I decided to move here when Reagan asked was because I needed a change. After college, I moved back to Memphis but it no longer felt like home especially after my parents died. I love my brother, but Rasheed has his own family and life with Bria. I needed a change of scenery, and when the opportunity presented itself I jumped on it. It wasn't supposed to be forever. I wanted to help Reagan and Zaria build their dream. They've discussed owning their own business since we were in high school, and yes, while I was saying it as well, I was going with the flow."

"So what is Brooklyn Vincent's dream career?"

"I still want to do photography but outside of the box which is why I'm excited about this new opportunity." She went on to explain the glass art book with Kameryn.

"Wow. A fascinating opportunity. I can read over the contract for you."

"That would be awesome. Thank you. I was going to send it to Rasheed's lawyer, but you're right here."

"Email it to me." He cited to her the email address as she typed it into her cellphone.

The waitress arrived with their food moments later, and they spent the next hour eating and reading over the contract. Chase made some minor changes she was in agreement with and sent it back to Kameryn's assistant.

Brooklyn was rather shocked she'd exposed her current feelings about her career to him. She was usually a private person and kept her thoughts and feelings bottled up; however, Chase was easy to talk to. Plus, he'd recently experienced something similar with changing careers. Same occupation but different avenue. However, now she would have to tell Reagan and Zaria of her plans with Kameryn as well as the possibility of leaving Precious Moments one day.

After dinner, they headed back to her home. Brooklyn had enjoyed her afternoon with Chase, but now as they were taking the camera equipment out of the golf cart, her heart had started to do crazy gymnastic flips whenever he was near. Little beads of perspiration had formed on the back of her neck, and while she could chalk it up to being in the warm garage, she knew her nerves were fizzling. She'd wanted nothing more than to kiss him, but thanks to her suggestion of taking things slow, she had to suffer in silence.

"I can take this up to your studio for you," he offered, hoisting the bag over his shoulder.

"Actually, it needs to go in the trunk of my SUV. I have a shoot tomorrow with Kam," she answered, clicking the trunk button on her key fob. The trunk of the Range

Rover raised, and he placed the bag next to the lighting ones already in there.

"I had a great time today. Thank you for the pictures. Now I can say I've done a professional photo shoot."

"Ha ha! Yes, you can add model to your already impressive resume. I'll email the pictures to you in a few moments so you can meet your deadline."

Shutting the trunk, he stepped toward her and pulled her into his arms. "Thank you. So was this our official first date?" he asked in a joking manner. Taking off his scarf, he placed it around her neck.

"You're funny," she replied, trying to laugh it off when she wanted to say yes and devour his lips with a follow up kiss. His embrace and scent drew an intoxicating mixture of uncanny emotions to ravage through her body. She had to ward off a shiver of goosebumps she sensed were going to prickle along her skin.

"Regardless of what we want to call it, I've enjoyed spending time with you these past couple of days. Something I've wanted to do for a long time."

"Me too." She kissed him on the cheek and backed out of his arms. "Good night, Chase."

"Kicking me out?" he questioned with a wink and headed toward the walkway leading to Addison's tiny home. "You have a date?"

"No. Precious Moments Events is having a meeting in an hour at Reagan's house," she said, checking her watch. "We usually meet for brunch on Mondays but our schedules were hectic today."

"Cool. I'm going to grade the pop quizzes."

"Don't be too hard on them, Professor Arrington," she reminded, waving a pointed finger at him. "Remember these scores don't count."

"I'll keep it in mind." Stuffing his hands in his front pockets, he turned on his feet toward his temporary home. "Have a great night."

"You too."

*****

"I still can't believe the three of you knew Blake was going to propose to me and didn't give me a hint or a heads-up," Reagan said with a teasing pout. "I was so surprised."

The ladies sipped peach wine spritzers, snacked on fruit, and relaxed in Adirondack chairs around the fire pit in the backyard of Reagan's home overlooking the Atlantic Ocean. The sun had set moments before and the ladies decided to enjoy the beach for their meeting which had turned into more of a social affair.

"Well, that was the whole idea," Zaria said. "However, you knew deep down he was going to propose. The man fell for you the moment you met."

"You weren't supposed to know." Brooklyn gave Reagan's upper arm a playful pinch. "The wedding planner with the commitment phobia finally finds the man to make her fall head over heels in love," she added in a sing-song tone.

Reagan held out her left hand to admire her three-carat, princess-cut engagement ring. "You're funny. Sounds like a tagline for a romance novel or a romantic comedy movie and I'm the heroine. But we've gotten off track, and the sooner we wrap up this meeting, I can go back to perusing Elle Lauren wedding gowns online even though I'm contemplating asking her to create a one of a kind dress. Z, you're up."

While Zaria began to go over her list of updates and concerns, Brooklyn found herself not listening. Not on purpose, but since her amazing day with Chase—or rather since he arrived at the engagement barbecue—she'd managed to tune out the world around her. Her thoughts wouldn't cease on Chase's charismatic charm, his laugh, his lips on hers, the way he stared at her with a promise in his eyes, which always jolted her heart into an overdrive of beats, and the moment when his glasses fogged up during their kiss. Even his scent had lingered in her memory. At least she assumed so until she realized she was still wearing his scarf when Addison gave her a questioning stare. But in her haste to email him the photos and arrive to the meeting on time, Brooklyn hadn't noticed it.

"Brook?" Reagan asked, glancing down at her notes. "What's going on with your schedule? Anything new?"

Leaving her daydream, Brooklyn grabbed her iPad from the table to read her schedule and notes. Now was the time to inform them of her other project with Kameryn. Her nerves were finding themselves sprinting through her veins at a rapid pace. Taking a deep breath, she decided to tell them about her opportunity with Kam but not mention the possibility of leaving the business because she honestly didn't know when she would take the leap.

"Yes, the photo shoot and interview is pretty much all day tomorrow and I have a wedding this weekend. Also, Kam has asked me to photograph some of her upcoming exhibits for the next year or so for a book she's creating of her glass art collections. I'll have to travel, but it will be mapped out around my schedule here. Luckily, we're not as busy in the fall as we are in the summer. In fact, I'm going to Memphis soon to shoot her glass collection at the Botanical Gardens."

"Oh, wow," Zaria exclaimed, raising her wine glass in the air in a toast. "To Brook for a wonderful opportunity. I know you've always enjoyed taking pictures outside of the box."

"Yes, indeed. So happy for you, as well," Addison said, clinking her glass with Brooklyn followed by Reagan. "Traveling is always fun."

"What wonderful news." Reagan set her glass down on the little table between her and Brooklyn. Standing, she reached down and hugged her best friend since elementary school. "And who knows, maybe you'll acquire more opportunities like this. You're such a creative photographer. Sometimes, I think you're wasting your talents and true calling here, but I'm so glad you're apart of Precious Moments. Now don't worry about any events which may come up while you're away, and we need a photographer. Your intern can handle it, or our backup photographers we've used at times."

Zaria joined in the hug as well. Brooklyn had been best friends with the Richardson cousins since they were all little girls growing up in the same neighborhood in the Frayser area of Memphis. During the difficult years of losing her parents, Zaria and Reagan were by her side through all the ups and downs as she'd done the same for them. Reagan had also experienced the heartache of her mother dying when she was four years old. Her father was in and out of her life but the two had recently reconciled.

"Also, on the accounting side of things, we're up to date with bills, and paychecks as always. No open invoices, and I did refund the Garden Association half of their deposit fee since they had to cancel their event for unforeseen circumstances. Does anyone have any questions from the detailed budget report I emailed this morning?"

"So, from glancing over it, I see there's room in the budget for us to have a booth at the Wedding Extravaganza Show in December?" Reagan asked. "We always acquire clients for the summer wedding season."

"Yes. I can do the registration for you and an intern to attend," Brooklyn answered, making a note. Brooklyn shut her iPad and tucked her feet underneath her in the chair. "If nothing else, Addi, it's your turn."

Addison sipped her wine, giving another glance at the gray scarf with a knowing gleam, and Brooklyn prayed she wouldn't say anything.

"All set for next week's Movie Night in the Park, and I booked a Christmas party with the Georgia United Teacher Association. I also have my friend's destination wedding on Hamilton Island, Florida next week. Can't wait. I've never been there before, but I hear the white sandy beaches are to die for. I hope I run into one of those fine Hamilton brothers," Addison said, with a wide grin. "Doesn't matter which one. They're all fine and dreamy."

"Yeah, girl. Caesar, Rome, and Lance are all handsome and *very* rich men," Zaria interrupted. "I admire how the Hamilton family has owned the island for decades and refuses to sell to anyone, but why would they? They're worth billions or so I heard."

"I love visiting there," Reagan said. "It's so neat how on one side of the island it's all hustle and bustle with high rise resorts and tourists everywhere. However, the other side it's such a sweet, charming beach town where all the locals literally know each other and welcome outsiders like family. Kind of like here I suppose, but with a quainter, small town feel. How are you traveling there? The closest major airport is in Pensacola."

"I was going to fly, but since Chase is checking out that weekend so to speak, I canceled my flight and hotel, and hitching up my tiny home to my truck. I already made campground reservations on the beach. So excited."

"Is his rental home almost ready?" Reagan asked with a swift glance at Brooklyn who sipped her wine in silence.

"Yep. I've enjoyed him, but I'm sure he wants his own space. You should see him climbing into the loft. Funniest sight you'll ever witness, but I'm glad he's stepped out of his comfort zone. Hunter sucked up all of the cool genes in the womb while Chase received all the seriousness. Lately, something has pulled Chase out of his always serious persona. Can't put my finger on it, but something or perhaps *someone* has tickled his fancy. Don't get me wrong, he still wants to play chess when I arrive home tonight. He's been in a lighthearted, relaxed mood since he arrived. Singing off key in the shower, whistling, and whatnot. I don't know. Maybe the change of scenery has helped."

Brooklyn let the words absorb in, especially the part about Chase moving into his rental home soon. Sadness surrounded her at the thought of not seeing him every day. And with Addison in and out of town, not to mention herself, when would she see Chase? Would he come all the way to the island if Addi wasn't there? She chastised herself for being bothered by it. They weren't in a relationship. They weren't dating. They were two people who had admired each other over the years, shared a kiss, and had agreed to learn about each other on a somewhat platonic basis.

Later on in the car ride home with Addison, who had ridden her bike to the meeting, Brooklyn tried to be cheery as she shared with her friend the life-like glass art animals Kameryn had designed.

"She's amazing," Addison said, scrolling through her cell phone before tossing it into her tote bag. "I'll definitely go to the exhibit when it opens. I love the idea of a coffee table book with her collections, but more so I am excited for you. How long will you be in Memphis?"

"For a couple of days, and a few weeks or so afterward Destin, Florida. Not sure where else. Waiting for Kameryn's assistant to send me the other locations."

"Mmm … I see. I'm sure my brother will miss you," Addison stated matter-of-factly, running a finger along the scarf. "Nice scarf."

"Addi, Chase is not going to miss me. We're … um …"

"Mmm-hmm. Exactly. I think you two are perfect for each other. I've known my brother for the last twenty something years and normally I don't concern myself with who he is dating. In fact, I'm still not. I have my own relationship woes, so I'm staying out of y'all business. You're both grown. But …"

"But? I thought you were staying out of grown folks' business," Brooklyn joked, turning into the driveway and pushing the button for the garage door to open.

"Ha! I'll start after this last comment. He sounded kind of reluctant when he mentioned his rental would be ready soon. I think he enjoys running into his neighbor. Trust me, he is not going to miss my tiny house, but I know he'll miss seeing you. There. I'm done." Addison made a zipline across her lips with two pinched fingers, jumped out of the SUV, and made her way to the bike rack on the trunk to retrieve her bicycle.

"Thank you." However, she knew Addi and this wouldn't be the end. "You know your Movie Nights in the Park are a hit," Brooklyn complimented, slamming the driver's side door and leaning on Addison's truck. She had to find a way to change the subject. "Sorry I'll miss this week's because of Kam's photo session, but I'll be there next week with my camera."

"Yes, the islanders have enjoyed it. Gives the tourists and locals something fun to do. I wish the lovebugs would skedaddle, but we have at least another month of them. I wanted to extend the movie night until the beginning of October since the weather is fabulous but the lovebugs are freaking everywhere. I'm tired of rinsing dead bugs off the hood and windshield of my truck every evening."

"Yeah, it can be a pain. I'll do mine in the morning," Brooklyn said, eyeing some on the grill of her vehicle.

"I thought they lived in Florida. This is Georgia."

"You know we're only an hour away from the state line. I kinda like the lovebugs, though," Brooklyn stated in a whimsical tone as she spotted some in the garage and shooed them out so she could close the garage door. "They're cute stuck together flying around. They are literally attached for life."

Addison swished her lips to the side as she hung her bike on the hook on the wall. "Only people 'in love' like lovebugs. Is someone falling in love? It would be cool to have you as a sister-in-law."

"Girl, stop." Brooklyn swatted her hand playfully at her friend. "Don't you have a chess match to attend?"

"You should come." Addison headed to the screen door in the garage adjacent to her tiny house. "I'm sure Chase would love to see you."

"No. I need to be up at the crack of dawn for Kam's photo shoot. Spend time with your brother before he goes back to Jacksonville."

"I've enjoyed his company but Jacksonville is only an hour away. Oh, before I leave for Hamilton Island, I need to stash my breakable items at your place to be on the safe side. I don't want any oopsies on the road."

"No problem. I didn't know you had anything breakable." Brooklyn remembered Addison had all plastic dishes and containers on purpose to avoid broken items while driving.

"A few crystal vases," Addison said with a shrug.

"Oh. I didn't realize you were into collecting vases."

"I'm not, but I received some lilies for my birthday and they were in a crystal vase. And then again last week ..." Addison's voice trailed off and she ran her fingers through her red waves of hair.

"A new love interest?" Thanks to being around brides in love, Brooklyn's keen sense of knowing when a woman was smitten with a man had risen. And there was indeed a sparkle in her friend's eyes at the mention of the flowers.

Addison smacked her lips and opened the door. "Goodness, no. An ex trying to worm his way back into my life. Not going to happen," she stated with a finger snap in the air. "I don't believe in second chances. Anyway, good night."

"Good night," Brooklyn answered with a light laugh as Addison left.

Brooklyn thought about Addison as she entered her home and headed straight to the master bathroom, flinging her clothes off along the way. Turning on the shower, she grabbed her shower cap from the hook next to the towel bar, hopped in, and let the cool water run over her before turning it toward the hot side.

Brooklyn didn't know Addison well before she'd moved to St. Simons to work for Precious Moments. She was Rasheed's cousin-in-law and had met her a couple of times. Addison had dated in the last year but no one had ever made it past a couple of dates for she was always on the go to some adventure. However, Brooklyn was rather surprised to see a glimmer and even a warm glow on Addison's face when she mentioned the ex; even if she didn't believe in giving him another chance she obviously had feelings for him. Still, she was only twenty-five and had plenty of time before settling down.

The thought brought Brooklyn to her current dating life. The one she didn't have. She'd dated a couple of nice guys since moving to St. Simons but none of them piqued her interests long enough to establish a real relationship. Like Addison, Brooklyn had some exes she would never go back to. Of course, none of them had tried and she had no reason to either. Then there was Chase, whose sexy smile and calming spirit she couldn't shake. He was indeed the epitome of everything she'd ever wanted in a boyfriend, possibly more, but in a few months he would be back in Memphis and she didn't know where her life would be.

Stepping out of the shower, Brooklyn dried off and proceeded to gather up the clothes she'd hastily flung on the floor. The notion of flinging them off for Chase filled her mind, causing a wicked smile to plaster on her face— especially when she grabbed his scarf which she purposely tossed on her vanity chair. She thought about giving it to Addison to return to him but decided against it. Besides, it had a faint lingering of his cologne mixed with his fresh scent, and as she drifted to sleep an hour later, she could smell the tantalizing scent as the scarf lay under her head.

Chapter Six

"You guys are naturals," Brooklyn complimented to a fun family of four that reminded her of her own close-knit family growing up. The dad was tall and handsome like her father with an attentive, caring nature toward his wife and two children. The mother was pretty and warm, reminding Brooklyn of her mother with a sweet personality. The son was the oldest at ten and seemed to take his role of big brother serious for his sister who was five and had tripped over her shoelaces when they were in line. He immediately picked her up, tied her shoes, and asked was she okay followed by offering her his ice cone. They'd attended the movie night a few weeks before and had returned to watch *Jurassic Park* to end their vacation before heading back to Connecticut in the morning, having spent the summer on St. Simons.

"Thank you," the mother answered. "My children loved the pictures from last time and wanted to do it again."

"Well, let's take one more for the road," Brooklyn said, noting the time on her watch and the line of people whose pictures she had to take before the movie began in thirty minutes. She was exhausted from a photo session with a bridal party and working on pure adrenaline, but had promised Addison she would do a photo booth as part of the pre-movie festivities that started two hours beforehand. Luckily, the music along with a candy bar had pepped her up a bit until she could eat the picnic dinner she'd packed.

She changed the green screen to reflect waves of ocean water, and the family of four did a surfing pose with the little boy pretending to fall over at the end. Laughing, she showed the mother the pictures on the computer and handed her a card with a number. "Take this to the young lady at the end of the booth. Your pictures will be printed momentarily. Have a safe trip home."

After they left, she continued with more families, children, couples, and individuals until she motioned to her photography intern, Kelli, to put the "Closed" sign up as the movie would begin soon.

"Whew, we're done," Kelli said, sipping her bottled water and sweeping her chestnut bangs away from her brow. "How many pictures did you take? A thousand?"

"Feels like it," Brooklyn answered, packing up their belongings. "I'm pleased with the turn out."

"Addison did a lot of advertising and *Jurassic Park* is a classic, you know."

"Yep. I remember watching it as a little girl with my family. Rasheed and I enjoyed it so much our parents took us back the next day."

She spotted the bouncy ponytail of Reagan's future sister-in-law, Parker Harrison-Sampson, along with her daughters, Lana and Bianca, in line at a food truck. Parker was dressed in khaki shorts and an Ocean World Escape T-shirt where she worked as a marine biologist. After handing her daughters some cash, she headed in Brooklyn's direction carrying a picnic basket as Kelli excused herself and finished packing the equipment.

"Hey, Brooklyn," Parker greeted, with a wide smile showing off her high cheekbones that would give supermodels a run for their money. Her honey-kissed skin had a slight tan from working outside all day training dolphins. "Thank you for sending me the pictures of the girls from the engagement barbecue."

"No problem. They had so much fun with their poses," Brooklyn responded with a hug. "Great to see you here." She noted a sadness about her, for even though Parker was smiling with her mouth, her almond-shaped eyes didn't display it. It was something Brooklyn had picked up on being a photographer.

"We barely made it. Traffic is jammed on the bridge from Brunswick to the island. I left work early to pick up the girls from school and run errands thinking I could beat the traffic. Now I'm ready to relax with a glass of wine," she sighed, patting the top of the basket.

"Geez. If you left Brunswick to drive to the girls' school in Jacksonville, Florida, and then back over here to the island, I'd say two glasses except you have to drive all the way back to Jacksonville again."

Parker's face scrunched into a melancholy of emotions as she shook her head. "No. Actually, I didn't go there. The girls and I live in Brunswick now. Closer to my job and my family." She paused as a wistful expression washed over her delicate features. "I filed for divorce from my soon-to-be ex earlier this summer and moved here a few weeks ago. We're staying on my parents' yacht at the marina until I move to Hamilton Island next year to work at the new Ocean World once its complete."

Brooklyn's hand flew to her mouth in an instant and she briefly glanced at Lana and Bianca who were laying out a blanket on the grass. "Oh, Parker. I know we don't know each other well so I had no idea. I'm so sorry. I just saw you two at the engagement barbecue last week." However, she remembered the couple barely spoke or even acknowledged each other. She assumed they'd had a disagreement like any other married couple.

"He showed up unannounced to see the girls, and *they* invited him to tag along. I don't want them to see us arguing. Trust me, I was ready to curse his trifling ass out, but at the same time I want him to see the girls as much as possible before we move. They aren't taking the divorce well. However, my family has been a wonderful support system."

"I'm so sorry you all are going through this," Brooklyn said, touching Parker's hand. "Perhaps you two may reconcile."

Parker pursed her lips. "No, I'm impatiently waiting for him to sign the papers. He's stalling over a hurt ego and shocked I actually filed and have moved on with my life. I thought he would be relieved so he could marry his side chick with the baby on the way and not have to sneak around anymore or lie about working overtime. But in the meantime, we co-parent our beautiful daughters. They're the only wonderful thing that came out of our marriage."

Dang, did she say side chick? A pregnant one at that. "Yes, your daughters are beautiful and so intelligent. Reagan is always saying how sweet and well-rounded they are." Brooklyn had decided to change the subject when she saw a tear form in the corner of Parker's eye.

"Ahh, yes. They're crazy about Auntie Reagan, as they now started to call her at the engagement party. They're ecstatic to be junior bridesmaids in the wedding. They were on the top deck practicing walking down the aisle last night." Parker paused, glancing in the girls' direction as Lana waved to her. They'd set up the blanket with their food and were laying down playing on their cellphones and snapping selfies. "Well, I'm going to settle in before the movie begins. Are you staying?"

Brooklyn wanted to jet home and sleep until the roosters crowed; however, she decided to stay when she spotted Chase earlier chatting with Addison. It had been a week since his photo session and their dinner at Brogen's. They'd seen each other in passing as both of their schedules had been hectic with his first week of school and Brooklyn had several events to leading up to a wedding with a weekend full of festivities.

"Yep. I think I'll stick around for a bit."

*****

"Wow, baby sis. I'm impressed with your event planning skills. Movie night is packed." Chase perused all the people in a variety of ages in the park gathering to see *Jurassic Park*. People were in low camp chairs, seated on picnic blankets, waiting in line at the numerous food trucks, or dancing to the music while they waited for the movie to start. He spotted Brooklyn when he arrived, but she was busy snapping pictures at the photo station. He was going to stop by and say hello but his sister put him to work setting up a few tents.

"I'm glad you think so, though *your* parents may not agree." Addison pointed a finger toward him as a solemn sadness washed over her features.

He hated their parents couldn't understand Addison was happy with her life choices. "*My* parents?" He chuckled at her usual sarcasm. "Still pestering you, huh?"

"I spoke to the Judge briefly this afternoon. He wanted to know if I had thought any more about law school."

"Ah … I see." He imagined their father, who they called the Judge, wearing a scowl across his face and his bald head that matched his and Hunter's probably displayed more creases than a pair of dress slacks. "Well, you did say you were doing a gap year before law school to travel… and it's been over three years."

Rolling her eyes up, Addison placed her hands on her hips. "I'm not interested. He thinks I'll eventually change my mind like Shelbi did when she wasn't sure about being a doctor. Uncle Frances wouldn't let up, and now neither will his brother. Is it an Arrington thing? Must we follow in our parents' footsteps? So because our cousins are all doctors like Uncle Frances and Aunt Darla, does that mean we all have to be lawyers like Mom and Dad? I wonder what Uncle Sean's children are going through … if he even had children." She shrugged, mentioning their uncle she barely knew. He'd been diagnosed with PTSD from serving in the Army and being on a few tours of duty which led him to commit suicide when she was a toddler. However, there had been rumors he possibly had children. Zoe had begun the research to find out if it was true in order to welcome them into the Arrington family.

"Something I wrestled with as well," Chase said in an empathetic tone. "I think it's one of the reasons why I left the firm the first time."

"But you were still a lawyer."

"True, but I wasn't happy being an ADA. It was very political. And that's the difference for me. I wasn't happy with my career change."

"And what if going back to Wentworth, Arrington, and Associates is a mistake?"

"Not this time. Mom is taking on more civil rights cases with the way of the world lately. It's something I'm passionate about. As far as your situation, I wouldn't worry too much. I think it's safe to say our parents know they raised a rebellious child, Journey."

"Whatever," she said, playfully punching Chase on the upper arm. "I don't believe in staying in one place for too long."

"Exactly. And speaking of, when are you leaving again for Florida?"

"Tuesday, and you're moving into your rental home this weekend?"

He sighed heavily at the reminder of this afternoon's conversation with the dean's secretary. "Yes and no. I'm moving back into the hotel this weekend."

"Why?"

"The rental has some type of an electrical issue now, but don't worry. I'll be fine. The department is footing the bill for the hotel. It's only for another week or so."

"Dang it. I shouldn't have cancelled my flight."

"No worries. I'll be fine. I'm a grown man."

"Mmm 'kay. I know you like stability, though. Tell you what. Stay this weekend and hang with me. I'm off on Saturday and Sunday. Go to the hotel on Monday. I gotta go check on a few things before the movie starts. Are you staying?"

"I hadn't planned to but ... um ... yeah, I am now." His eyes landed on Brooklyn once more as she hugged Reagan's future sister-in-law good-bye.

"Mmm-hmm. Enjoy." Addison skipped away in the direction of the DJ's booth.

"I definitely will," Chase answered, placing his focus on Brooklyn who had returned to packing up her equipment and setting it in the trunk of the golf cart. She gave her assistant a hug and swiped a blanket and tote bag from the backseat. The intern drove off on the golf cart, and Brooklyn pivoted in his direction wearing a knowing smile as if she knew his attention had been on her the entire time.

*****

Brooklyn had an inkling she was being watched by a pair of seductive eyes when she was chatting with Parker. She sensed a penetrating warmth on her bare legs had roamed up to the hem of her chambray shirt dress, to the brown leather belt cinched at her waist, up to her breasts which had hardened at the notion of being admired by Chase, followed by a breathtaking touch on her neck and then lingered on her lips like the taste of chocolate. Brushing a lock of her hair, which had fallen out of her messy, clipped updo, she shifted her weight to the other leg as Chase approached. A gust of wind streamed over his woodsy scent to her atmosphere even before he reached her. It was more pronounced and stronger than she'd remembered which Brooklyn chalked up to the fact she'd noticed him helping Addison with some last minute tasks. And she was thankful because catching glimpses of his upper arm muscles flexing while setting up a tent was the overall adrenaline she needed to stay awake.

He was casually dressed in khaki cargo shorts and a short-sleeved shirt similar to her dress. His bald head she'd fantasized gliding a sensual hand over was unfortunately covered with a Memphis Grizzlies cap, and for a moment it made her homesick. His glasses were missing and she couldn't but help miss them as she remembered the way they'd steamed up during their kiss. Her eyes zeroed in on the five o'clock shadow gracing his face with a sexual presence causing her to shift her weight to the other leg and take a slight step backwards as he landed in her personal space.

"Hi there," Chase greeted, moving the wisps of hair which had fallen over her eye again back behind her ear. "I've been trying to make it over here for the past hour, but Addi put me to work as soon as I arrived."

"She's good at that." Brooklyn paused for a moment, contemplating whether or not to ask him if he was staying for the movie. "Are you staying to watch the dinosaurs take over the world?"

"Yeah. I gotta go grab my camp chair out of the car."

"Oh …my blanket is king size. We can share." *Wait! Those words spilled out of my mouth a little too naturally.*

Stepping toward her, he took the blanket out of her arms. "I accept the invite. I don't mind being wrapped up in a blanket with you." Winking, he turned to peruse the area.

His voice was deep and low, sending a wave of heat to caress over her skin as if it were his hands. Glancing around the park, she prayed no one noticed her cheeks were on fire and would spray cold water on her.

"Thank you for the vision," she said, scanning where they could set up as well as avoiding eye contact with him. The park was crowded but there were a few spaces left including the one in front of the photo booth which had a perfect view of the screen and out of the way of the crowds.

"Quite welcome. Perhaps one day it won't be a vision."

"You don't quit, do you?"

"Because you don't want me to," he answered in a seductive and serious tone.

"I'm ignoring you. How about we set up here?"

"Sounds good."

Moments later the blanket was spread out on the grass, and they were seated next to each other. Brooklyn kicked off her sandals, something she'd wanted to do since the photo session earlier in the day, and opened her tote bag.

"I have plenty of food. Reagan was supposed to join me but she's having dinner with Blake to discuss wedding dates." Brooklyn set out containers of her homemade curry chicken salad, a shrimp pasta salad, blackberries, croissants, and a mixture of cashews and pecans. Taking out two thermoses along with two plastic red cups, she handed one to Chase. "Do you drink? If not, I have bottled water, as well."

"Sure, bartender. What do you have?"

"One is a Georgia peach margarita, and in the other thermos is a watermelon mojito. Addi made them."

"What a variety of girlie drinks. No, Jack Daniels or Hennessy?" he teased with a wink. "I'll have the margarita."

After they fixed their plates, making sure to save some for Addison, they ate quietly while watching the beginning of the movie. Since it was an outdoor event, people were still talking amongst themselves considering the speakers were loud enough so no one could complain about the noise as if in a theater.

"How are you enjoying St. Simons?" she asked.

"I like it. Being on the island makes me feel as if I'm on vacation even though I have to be at work in the morning. I'm going to miss being here though."

"Oh, yeah." Her voice cracked, and she immediately sipped her margarita. "Addi mentioned you were moving out this weekend. But it's good your rental is ready." *Not really but I'm not going to relay that information.* "I can't even imagine you climbing up in the guest loft every night."

"No, it now has an electrical issue. I found out before leaving work. I'm moving back into the hotel near campus on Monday since Addi is leaving Tuesday."

"Oh, wow. I'm so sorry. They don't have another visiting professor home?"

Chase sighed as his face scrunched in frustration. "Nope. All taken. No big deal." He shrugged. "Besides, the hotel has free breakfast, snacks and cocktails in the evenings, plus housekeeping. I'll be fine. It's only for a week. I've been meaning to ask you, how did the contract changes go?"

"Kam accepted them, and I fly out to Memphis on Saturday morning. Were you able to turn your bio picture in on time?"

"Yes. I appreciate the last minute photo session."

"Anytime," she answered sincerely. "You're family."

"For the record, we're not related. I may be your sister-in-law's cousin, but I repeat, we are not related. Unless, of course …" a snarky grin inched up his left cheek and he whispered in her ear, "you want to marry me one day."

The subtle yet on purpose touch of his lips on the bottom of her lobe zapped an electric current to straight to her center. Her eyes shut for a second and she turned her head toward him, praying her tone would be even considering now his lips were a mere inch from hers."I was referring to Addi being like a little sister to me."

"She will be when we're married," he stated in a serious tone. "Just let me know where you want to go on the honeymoon."

"You're a mess," she quipped, trying to ignore the flutters in her stomach.

"When you want something, you speak it into existence."

"Marriage?" She laughed it off, but the thought of walking down the aisle to him, raising children and growing old together played in her head like a movie. "We haven't even been on a date."

"I beg to differ. We had dinner at Brogen's, and now we're at movie night."

"Um ... it wasn't a date, and technically I'm at work. And so are you. You know Addi will want you to take the tent down, right?" she reminded.

"Of course. Soooooo ... have any plans Friday? I don't have classes but I have office hours in the morning. I've been so busy, I haven't had a chance to experience island life."

"I'm free Friday afternoon."

"So it's a date?"

"No, but we can hang out. Remember, we agreed to be friends ...without benefits," she added, even though she could still feel the warmth of his lips on hers, and craved for them to be there once more.

"Only time will tell."

"You're funny, and since you want the 'island experience,' I have a few ideas you may enjoy."

"Cool. I look forward to our da– hanging out."

"Hey." Addison plopped down on the other end of the blanket and grabbed a bottled water from the tote bag. "What did I miss?" She pulled out the pasta salad, spooned a few forkfuls on a paper plate, and took some of the blackberries. "You two look like something mischievous is going on." Taking a bite of the salad, she studied both of them carefully.

Brooklyn and Chase glanced at each other with a knowing smile, and then at Addison who was popping berries into her mouth with one hand while tapping her fingers of the other hand on the blanket.

"What's with the secret look?" Addison asked, placing her gaze on her brother. "You know I'm observant, Chase."

"Nothing."

"Well, if you say so. I won't pry. But you'll be happy to know you can stay in my house after all. I've decided to rent a RV van. Something I've wanted to do for awhile now." Standing, Addison took a swig of her bottled water. "Perfect. The park manager has finally arrived, and I need to speak with him." She headed in the direction of the man who had signaled for her attention.

"I guess I'll be hanging around for another week on the island," Chase said as a naughty smile plastered across his face.

Instead of answering, Brooklyn stuffed the rest of the pasta salad into her mouth and placed her focus on the screen. She hated to admit she was ecstatic he'd be there awhile longer, but she wasn't going to tell him.

"Your silence means you're happy I'm staying after all."

"Nope. I just like this scene in the movie." She pivoted her head toward him and winked.

"Mmm-hmm. I know you're looking forward to it, as I am. Especially our date."

"Hanging out," she corrected. "And I'm going to give you an island experience you'll never forget."

"Really?" He scooted closer until his lips were back on her ear. "Care to elaborate?"

A sensual sensation prickled along her body as his tongue had deliberately flicked across her skin and was lingering, waiting for her to answer. She'd imagined his tongue on other parts of her body and the desire to experience it ripped through her. For a moment, she wanted to forget they were in public so she could turn her head and place her lips on his to satisfy the hunger of the kiss she'd longed for ever since the last one. Brooklyn promised herself not to give into temptation but some promises were meant to be broken. Especially one as tempting as Chase Arrington. She decided right then and there that whatever happens, happens and there would be no regrets from her.

"I guess you'll just have to be patient and find out," she said, moving away from him before she'd let him find out right now, and they'd be arrested for lewd conduct in the park.

"Can't wait, beautiful."

*****

Later on that night, Brooklyn lay awake thinking about the events of her life which had transpired in two weeks. Never in a million years had she imagined he felt the same way. Maybe there was some truth in what Chase said about speaking things into existence. Had she said it out loud? She couldn't remember. However, the more she thought about some of the things she prayed for lately, she realized they had happened—such as a different career path and finding a good man. Chase definitely was a good man. Almost too good, but she had an inkling her two guardian angels were watching over her as they always had. It was something both her parents had promised her and Rasheed they would do when they were on their death beds. The thought of them not being there strained her heart and melancholy filled her being. At one point she didn't want a wedding because if her father couldn't give her away and her mother couldn't be there to help her plan and prepare, she didn't want to. However, she was a teenager at the time, and as she grew older, she knew her big brother would have no problem doing the honor and Reagan along with Zaria would be by her side fussing over her hair and makeup.

Brooklyn wiped a few stray tears and let out a soft giggle over her two best friends being more of a mess than she would on her wedding day. She didn't even know why she was thinking of her wedding day. Thanks to Chase joking about them marrying, she had conjured up crazy thoughts and images. She even pictured tossing her bouquet to Addison who clearly didn't seem as if she wanted to settle down anytime soon. She laughed out loud at Chase's marrying joke but then it died down as something in her gut screamed he wasn't kidding.

Turning off the lamp on the nightstand, Brooklyn slid under the comforter for some type of comfort and to hopefully shield the fact he was indeed serious and apart of her didn't mind at all.

Chapter Seven

"So you think us dying on our first date is a great idea?" Chase asked as they stood on the dock of We Love to Parasail. "How utterly romantic." He shoved his hands in the pockets of his swim trunks and stared down at Brooklyn with a smirk. If she wasn't so damn sexy in her purple bikini, and the fact it was her and not some random chick he barely knew, he would jump in his ride and leave.

"You said you wanted to experience island life," she reminded.

"Well at least you have some experience. The crew on the boat waved to you like you're a regular. How many times have you parasailed?"

"Um ... no. I've never been either. I know them because I was the photographer at their wedding this summer."

The popping of a vein on his forehead was imminent. "Wait. What? This is your first time, too?" He tried to keep his tone steady but a sense of nervousness washed over him.

"Surprise," she answered with a bashful smile. "We can experience it together."

"Well, there are some things I wouldn't mind us experiencing together ..." he started, sliding his hands around the indent of her waist. He wanted to lower his lips to hers, but he was trying hard to be a gentleman and stick to their agreement which flew out the window every time they were near each other. "You know, I think parasailing will be fun. It's different." He was more so convincing himself. He could hear his other sister, Zoe, in his head shouting at him to "man up."

"Perfect. I have to admit I'm sort of scared but it's something I've wanted to do since moving here. I didn't have anyone I trusted to keep me safe ... until you arrived."

"I got you. You're safe with me."

"I'll keep that in mind."

They waited in line for a few more moments watching other people on their parasailing adventure. Chase stood behind her with his arms still wrapped around her body and his chin resting on the top of her hair. He was shocked she didn't protest, but he could sense her nervousness and probably didn't mind the comfort of him next to her even though he was a tad nervous as well. He wanted to plant amorous kisses on Brooklyn's neck and shoulders, but instead he tried to place his focus on the Atlantic Ocean and not the fact her plump bottom rested on him ever so perfectly. Every part of her body fit snug against him as if she were molded for him. Perhaps a rib had been taken from his body to create the flawlessness which was Brooklyn Vincent for she was the first woman he'd ever said the word marriage to. While he was joking, there was something in the way he said it that came from a place deep within. It was as if he meant it and Chase wasn't scared of that fact. Brooklyn's face had softened into a beautiful array of emotions when he'd spoke it into existence, but the one emotion not present was fear. Sure, she laughed it off but she didn't object, and the thought made him sneak in a quick peck to the side of her neck.

The cute giggle, followed by her intertwining her fingers with his, made him realize even more he could definitely see himself standing where he was with her nestled in his arms for infinity.

"We're up next," he whispered as the couple in front of them prepared to put on their life jackets since another couple had returned.

Peering at him over her shoulder, Brooklyn formed her lips in a cute pout. "Is it too late to change my mind?"

Squeezing her gently, he rocked her in his arms to ease her nerves. "Too late."

Moments later they were given safety instructions and signed a waiver release form. They continued watching the couple in front of them until they found themselves on the parasailing boat putting on their life jackets and safety harness swing they would sit in.

"Ready?" Chase asked, as the newlyweds, Sunni and Jake, hooked the harnesses to the parasail and they sat as if on a playground swing.

"Yep," Brooklyn replied, gripping the swing. "No turning back now."

"All right," Jake started. "Going to release you two. Hold on."

Clenching the swing tight, Chase leaned over and kissed Brooklyn on the lips as the parasail released them backwards up in the air five hundred feet above the water. They both screamed and laughed at the same time, dangling their legs.

"Oh my goodness," she shouted. "I can't believe we're doing this."

"Woo hoo!" He panned his phone around to video the scenery. "The view is amazing."

"It is. So glad you brought your phone. I was scared I'd drop mine, but now I wish I had my camera."

"The boat and the crew are wayyyyyyyy down there." He pointed down at the boat pulling them. "This is insane."

"It is. Aren't you glad I thought of this?"

"I am, but I didn't care what you planned. I want to continue our journey of learning about each other."

"Sweet of you to say." A grin spread across her cheeks. "So you're down with swimming with the sharks next?" she asked jokingly.

He jerked his head quick toward her. "Don't push it, woman."

"I'm kidding, but this is truly the coolest thing I've ever experienced. Look how beautiful and serene the water is."

"It is breathtaking. The best way to view it. Oh, there's the lighthouse."

"And look, is that Brogens?"

They enjoyed the next few minutes pointing out other landmarks around the island and taking a few selfies.

"I could stay up here all day," Brooklyn said with a sigh. "I hate our time is almost up."

"Me too." He nodded in agreement as they were being lowered back to the boat. "This was the fastest twenty minutes. I guess time does fly when you're having fun."

"But our day isn't over yet," she stated in a sing-song tone. "I have one more water adventure planned."

He noted her mischievous expression. "I'm almost scared to ask what's next."

"You'll see momentarily," she said, fluttering her eyelashes in an innocent manner and patting his knee.

And he did. They headed over to the cycle boat dock, and he was relieved it wasn't skydiving. Afterwards, they picked up a late lunch/early dinner at Brogens and decided hang out on Coast Guard Beach. It was full with tourists and locals, but they were able to find a spot away from the crowds to set up the camp chairs and an umbrella.

"I can get used to driving around in a golf cart," Chase commented, standing to fix the umbrella they'd buried in the sand. The wind had picked up a bit since they'd arrived. "Think I could drive a cart in downtown Memphis?"

"Probably not," Brooklyn replied, crinkling her nose. "One of the things I'll miss if I ever leave the island."

"Still deciding?" Chase sat back down and took a bite of his turkey burger. Her faraway, wistful expression had him regretting the question. He didn't want to ruin the day with her thinking about her present career issue. He'd been there before when he considered leaving his last position.

Sighing, she dipped a sweet potato fry into the honey mustard. "Yeah ... I'm looking forward to going home tomorrow and working with Kam on her book project. I'm still in limbo about leaving Precious Moments, and I haven't told Reagan and Zaria yet of my dilemma. But I can't worry about it at the moment. I'm glad you enjoyed parasailing and the cycle boating."

He was relieved she changed the subject. "The cycle boating was a great cool down from the adrenaline high of parasailing."

"And I got a nice leg work out, too" she said, rubbing her thighs and tucking her legs underneath her in the chair. "Now I don't have to feel bad about missing the gym today."

Chase was disappointed when she removed her long, tanned legs from his view. He'd been admiring their softness and had to restrain himself from reaching over to caress them.

"You know there's skydiving over in Jacksonville," he teased. "Could be our next hang out when you return."

"Now that's something I wouldn't do and apparently not you either. I saw you at your cousin Preston's skydiving wedding. You were on the ground with the rest of the bystanders who didn't want to jump with the bride and groom. I was relieved one of the skydivers accompanying them took the pictures."

"Oh, so you were checking me out at their wedding?" He rubbed his hand over on his chin and peered down at her over his shades. "I'm flattered."

She glanced away from him. "No, not what I said."

"Honestly, I thought about it, but I'm not a dare devil like Preston. He and Addi are the family's adrenaline junkies ... well, we aren't actually blood-related to the Chase family, but we say we're cousins since we share the other set of Arringtons."

"Oh, I see. I guess I never realized that. I only know Bria and Shelbi. So how did you get the name Chase?" Brooklyn wrapped her hair in a bun at the top of her head as the wind picked up a bit more.

"My Aunt Darla's maiden name is Chase. My mom thought it would be a cool first name. She didn't want rhyming or similar names for Hunter and I."

"Must be cool to have a twin."

"It is. He's my best friend and we love being big brothers to Addi and Zoe."

"You all seem so close. I love the dynamics of a big family. It was just me and Rasheed growing up, but along with the Richardsons and the Martins, we're all one big circle of friends. Our parents were all best friends growing up as well, and hopefully my children will be friends with their children."

"Ah ... so you want kids one day." It was more of a statement than a question. Usually discussing children would have him sprinting away, but with Brooklyn he was completely at ease.

"I do, and apparently with you since we're gonna be hitched and all," she teased, pinching him on the arm.

"Yep." Leaning over, he kissed her tenderly on the side of her neck. "Sounds like a plan."

Letting out an aroused moan, she swiped her water bottle from the cup holder in the chair and took a long swig. "You play too much." Pausing, Brooklyn stood and pointed out to the sea. Grabbing her camera from her tote bag, she moved closer to the water. "It's a family of dolphins."

"Nice. Real nice," he complimented, hoping she wouldn't turn around and realize he wasn't commenting

76

on the dolphins but instead her shapely body in the bikini. She had to be the same measurements as in the song "Brick House" by the Commodores. She had the most bouncy breasts he'd ever seen, and the bikini top enhanced their jiggle even more. Her tiny waist, which he'd enjoyed wrapping his arms around, offset her clutchable hips and plump butt was all natural from eating southern soul food and squats. He was somewhat jealous of her bikini bottom for having the lucky chance to be directly attached to her.

Pivoting on her heel, Brooklyn snapped a picture of him. "You sure are wearing a sexy smize, mister."

"Oh, really?" He shifted in his seat and tried to relax his face.

"Yeah. What naughty thoughts are going on in that brain of yours?"

Dang, was it obvious? "Nothing." He shrugged, taking a sip of his cool water. "I'm admiring the exquisite view." *There. It wasn't a lie*

"The dolphins?" she asked, snapping another picture of him and sitting back down.

Chase took the last bite of his burger and chewed slow as she eyed him with pressed lips.

"Oh … um … sure. The dolphins."

*****

Brooklyn began to giggle at his lie and tossed a French fry at him. She knew he was checking her out the entire time, especially when she'd slipped off her sarong before parasailing. Chase's breath had sucked in and the same sexy smize from a moment ago was plastered on his face as if he'd hit the jackpot. She could always sense his intense stare on her. It heated her body like a blow torch firing upon crème brûlée. However, he wasn't the only one as she found herself stealing glances at him through her dark shades. His bare chest glistened from the sun screen and a film of sweat settled on his chocolate-kissed skin. Chocolate had always been her weakness, and fighting off the urge to straddle his lap to kiss him couldn't shake out of her thoughts. Brooklyn felt somewhat bad for her naughty way of thinking considering she was the one pushing the "stay friends" narrative. However, they'd already had their first kiss along with a few stolen kisses which basically had her wanting to scream, "Take me now."

"I'm thinking about taking a swim in thirty minutes after my food digests. You wanna join me?" Chase asked after he returned from throwing their trash in the garbage.

"I'd love to."

Thirty minutes later, they rode the waves together, got knocked over a few times, had a water splash fight all while laughing their asses off and stealing kisses in-between.

"Okay, time-out," Brooklyn said, exhaling and making a T-sign with her hands. "I need to catch my breath." Winking, she splashed water on him as he proceeded to grab her to his chest. She wrapped her arms around his neck and was about to kiss him when a sharp pain on the bottom of her leg had her shrieking in pain.

"Ouch! What was that?" Eyeballing her leg, she spotted a jellyfish attached to it and started to kick her leg until Chase grabbed the pest and flung it back into the ocean.

"Are you okay, babe?" he asked, scooping her up in his embrace, carrying her ashore and laying her down on the blanket spread out in front of their camp chairs. "I'll pour some ice water on the sting." He reached over to the mini ice chest, grabbed a bottled water, and poured it over the bite. Placing cubes in a clean napkin from their meal, Chase set it on the area and held it.

"I'm fine. It happens. I have some meat tenderizer in my beach bag."

His forehead indented into an awkward, puzzled position. "Meat tenderizer? You plan on catching it and frying it? Is it some kind of island ritual?"

Chuckling at the seriousness of his question, she rummaged around in her tote and pulled out the container and opened it. "No, silly. You sprinkle it on the sting. It takes the pain away, but the ice is helping as well." She handed it to him and he shook the seasoning over the sting.

She was impressed by Chase's caring nature and appreciated his attentiveness as he stroked her wet hair with an expression of concern plastered on his face. It reminded Brooklyn of her father who always showed concern especially when her mother grew weak in the end, and he did his best to make sure she was comfortable until her last breath.

"Well, relax," he said softly. "I'm here."

"Okay." Closing her eyes, she let her focus go to the comfort of his touch and not the burning sensation of the sting. Luckily, there wasn't a tentacle left on her leg to remove. She'd experienced that before and the pain was unbelievable.

"Looks like people are getting out of the water because of the jellyfish," Chase said moments later. "A few other people got stung as well and are leaving."

She opened her eyes to his empathetic gaze on her. "There's never only one of them. We should probably head out as well. The tide will be on the shore soon."

"I'll take everything to the golf cart. You lie here and rest."

Sitting up, she shook her head. "I can help. I'm fine."

Standing, he began to fold up the camp chairs and place them back in their covers. "Nope." He bent down and kissed her tenderly on the cheek. "I got this, Brook."

Ten minutes later, Chase placed her tote bag on his shoulder and lifted Brooklyn into his arms.

"I can walk, you know," she stated as he made the trek on the sand to the parking lot.

"Nonsense."

"All right now. I can get used to being treated like a queen."

"That's the whole idea."

Chapter Eight

"I don't feel comfortable leaving you," Chase called out from the kitchen, placing ice cubes into a ziplock bag to make an ice pack. Brooklyn had taken a shower and was resting on the chaise lounge in the sitting area of her house. Walking through the hallway to the kitchen, he noticed the black and white photographs framed in red frames on both sides of the wall of flowers, glass art, and other photographic art from around the island. He didn't know anything about photography but the angles and lighting of the photos were creative and engaging. They belonged in an art gallery for patrons to admire and buy.

"I'm fine. I rubbed some ointment on it. It wasn't a bad sting. You threw him off before he could do any real damage. I've been stung before, and trust me, it was much worst."

He sat on the edge of the chaise next to her leg which was propped up on a pillow and set the ice pack on the sting. "Is there anything I can do? Do you need help packing?"

"No. I packed this morning, but you can keep me company for a bit."

"Tell you what," he said, standing and glancing at his watch. "You rest here, and I'm going to run home and take a quick shower. Be back in twenty minutes."

"You do smell like the ocean," she teased, wrinkling her nose. "I'll rest a bit."

"Don't go anywhere until I return. While you were in the shower, I read online there are allergic reactions including hives, nausea, vomiting, or stiffness from jellyfish stings."

"All of which would've happened by now," she reassured, rubbing his hand and placing a kiss on his cheek. "I'm fine."

"Gotcha. I'll be back."

Stretching her arms over her head, she rested against the chaise. "I'll be here."

Chase headed through the kitchen and to the path to Addison's house. He found her on the couch reading a book on RV van living and sipping a huge mug which had the word "TEA" monogrammed on it in all caps. A bouquet of orange lilies were on the kitchen island, but he decided not to say anything for he knew who they were from.

Closing it, she set the book on the couch. "Hey, lover boy. Back so soon? She realized you have no swag?" she joked.

"Ha, ha. No. I'm taking a quick shower and heading back."

"Mmm-hmm." Waving her hand in front of her nose, Addison sniffed and pinched her nose with two fingers. "You do smell kinda fishy. You know there's an outdoor shower attached on the other side of my house."

"You got jokes. But seriously, Brooklyn was stung by a jellyfish so I want to make sure she doesn't break out in hives or something."

"If she hasn't broken out yet she won't," Addison reassured, tilting her head and swishing her lips to the right side. "Ah ha. You aren't ready to say goodnight. I know how you men operate."

Chase noted a slight annoyance with Addison's last comment, and her eyes briefly darted to the flowers.

"Now take your shower and go hang out with my friend, but don't stay too late. We're waking up early in the morning to go deep sea fishing with Zaria and Garrett. I believe Reagan and Blake are tagging along as well."

"Cool. That sounds like fun."

"And I have a surprise for you afterwards," Addison called out as he headed toward the bathroom.

Twenty minutes later—after a refreshing shower—he dashed back to Brooklyn's. Locking the patio door, he called out to her as he strolled to the sitting area. Chase found her sleeping peacefully in the same spot cuddled in a ball. The ice pack was on the floor and the swelling had gone down. Her black T-shirt dress rested above her thighs, causing a groan to stir from him as he spotted matching boyshorts hugging where he longed to caress. Stooping next to her, he tousled her hair that had dried into a curly, lion's mane, making her golden highlights more pronounced.

"Mmm," Brooklyn moaned softly and opened her eyes. "Hi," she said, with a lazy smile. "You're back."

"Hey, Sleeping Beauty."

"I wasn't asleep," she answered with a light yawn. "Just dozing."

"We've had a long day," he said, continuing to stroke her hair. "But I had a wonderful time today. I didn't want it to end."

The cinnamon flakes in her eyes darkened and her voice lowered to a seductive whisper. "Who said it has?"

A surprised smile smoothed across his face at the obvious turn of events. Seizing her to him, Chase brushed his lips against hers like a paint brush on a fine canvas, which caused a sensual purr to escape her throat. He submerged deeper when her hands encircled his neck and

Brooklyn met his erotic kisses match for match. The passion which exuded from her articulated without words, and like him, a case of pent-up desire which had lingered since their first kiss. Her hands roamed from his neck, down to his chest, and dove under his shirt to caress his abs before gliding sensually around his waist to settle on his back. Brooklyn groaned in frustration, gripping her hands on his skin.

"I could take it off," he suggested. "Or you can …" His voice trailed off with widening eyes at her sudden movement to do so.

Pulling up the shirt, snatching it over his head, and tossing it on the floor was her response. Yanking him to her, she wrapped her legs around his waist and continued the exquisite bliss on his lips. Her dress rose above her hips, and he could feel the warmth of her nestled against him. Brooklyn's in-control habits were a turn-on since their first kiss. Never had a woman made him feel such emotion and vigor this early in a relationship, but he'd always sensed a kindred attraction to her since the first moment their eyes connected years ago. It had never dwindled, and now had exploded into a powerful existence between them that was displayed in the way they kissed, touched, and occasionally opened their eyes to glance at the other followed by a knowing smile.

Chase's lips left hers, trailing an ardent path along the side of her neck and down to where her dress met the top of her cleavage. However, instead of continuing, he slid his tongue up to the other side of her neck, as the sweetest whisper of his name peeked from her lips. It was a symphony to his ears, which encouraged him to nibble, lick, and gently bite her neck while clenching her butt with his hands. The sensual rotation of her hips and her fingertips digging in his back, which was sure to leave a few marks, knocked him over the edge into a state of an amorous oblivion. If Brooklyn was this passionate with casual foreplay, he couldn't even imagine if they were naked and intertwined together making love. A growl flowed from him at the thought, and her sliding her hand over his head to catch his lips with hers informed him she was all on board. They were in total oneness with each other, and the more they kissed, the more he wanted and needed all of her.

*****

Once again Brooklyn was on an adrenaline high that day; however, this one soared higher than their parasailing adventure. The overzealous state she was currently swept into, had filled her with unfamiliar emotions she desired to explore more of. Chase's ardent kisses and moans caused her to erase the willpower she strived to have around him. She couldn't help it. His presence always caused her to let down her guard no matter how hard she tried to maintain it. She'd tossed and turned at night dreaming about the man who kissed her as if she had always belonged solely to him. He'd erased all the other men from her past and the thought of any other man in the future constricted her heart into an uncanny pain. Brooklyn couldn't imagine anyone but Chase holding her, gazing at her, taking care of her, or kissing her the way he did.

Settling her head back against the toss the pillow he'd placed under her head, she let him carry her away on a journey of ecstasy as he kissed along her neck and collarbone. She wanted him to go further and had practically begged him, saying his name over and over along with clutching his bare shoulders. How many more hints did she need to give? The warmth of his skin penetrated through her dress and onto her skin, but she yearned to feel him against her. She removed his hand from her bottom and glided it down to her dress. Raising an eyebrow, he understood her silent plea and in one swoop the dress was discarded next to his shirt on the floor to expose she was braless.

"Beautiful," he whispered. "All of you is remarkably beautiful."

Biting his bottom lip, he sucked one of her nipples into his mouth, winding his tongue around it in a slow, sensual pace.

"Mmm ... Chase, you're so perfect." She shut her eyes and concentrated her mind on the feel of his tongue teasing both of her breasts while his hand massaged the top of her panties in the same sensual rhythm. Her hips began to follow suit an unhurried pace, and her breathing unraveled with every moan released from her. Brooklyn clenched his shoulders as he sped up a tad, and she didn't know how much more she could handle before she reached her peak. Being with Chase in this manner was the greatest place on Earth; better than Disney World. No ride or attraction there could compare to the roller coaster of emotions he had her on.

His lips reached hers once more after driving her breasts insane for leaving them. He weaved his hand into her hair while mingling his tongue with hers in a wild, heightened kiss. Their satisfied sounds filled the atmosphere and drowned out any common sense jarring around in Brooklyn's head. His hands along her skin tormented her even more. The fork in the road between love and lust was present, and the more he continued to make her feel like the only woman in the world, the more she had to realize she was simply trying to live in the moment of the feelings which started eight years ago.

Chase halted their kiss abruptly and held onto her tighter than he had during their entire tryst. Her eyes flew open to find him in an intense, serious stare. His clenched jaw showcased his sculptured face and his breathing had increased even though they were still. A finger lingered on the waistband of her panties, and she knew the question he was asking without uttering a single word.

Goodness, she'd daydreamed about this very second for years. Her desire for Chase sped rampant in her veins like race cars zooming around the track nonstop. The only way to calm her down would be to give into temptation and the curiosity of being one with him. Brooklyn had yearned to know the feeling of him inside of her, joining their bodies and minds until they couldn't tell where the other one began and ended. She craved him not on a physical aspect but mentally and spiritually. She knew there was so much more to what they shared besides a physical attraction. Chase was the man she pictured a future with by the way he stared at her, smiled at her, or his attentiveness to her needs. It was one of those whirlwind romances she'd read about in romance novels which always ended in a happily-ever-after. But would hers end happily? Chase would be moving back to Memphis in December and she had no idea where she would be career wise or city wise. Panic rose in her, and the thought of him not being in her life one day shattered through her like broken glass. However, starting a relationship with him would be naïve on her part. How did she possibly think it had been a good idea in the first place? Still didn't mean she couldn't finally have her vivid daydream of being with him intimately come true. *You only live once,* she thought.

"Chase," she began, placing her hand on his face, "I think we should …"

"Wait?" he asked, sliding off of her and grabbing his shirt from the floor. Handing Brooklyn her dress, he slipped on his shirt. "I guess we got kinda carried away. *Again.* We have plenty of time," he stated matter-of-factly, caressing her hair.

Standing, she kissed him softly on the lips and proceeded to take his shirt off and fling it across the room. "No. I think we should go to my bedroom."

"Are you sure? I don't want you to regret this in the morning."

"The only thing I regret is not doing this sooner but … only this *one* night," she stated seriously.

He cracked a sexy, arrogant grin, lifted her into his arms, and began to walk to her bedroom. "One night is all

I need to make you mine," he said, resting his forehead against hers.

"I'm serious. I can't promise anything past tonight."

"Then you may want to rethink this, babe, considering you're already halfway addicted to me. One night and trust me, you're going to want … no, *need* more."

"Well, the same can be said about you as well, mister. But we're adults. We know exactly what this is and what it can't be. So tonight only."

"We'll see about that," he said, winking as he entered the room and lowered her onto the plush gold comforter with him following on top of her.

The seriousness in his tone and the way his lips crashed on hers with an intense possessiveness he'd never displayed before with her, sent her heart racing as a shiver cascaded down her spine. In an instant, Brooklyn knew he was right. She would crave more because in that moment her heart was indeed all his, and she never wanted to be without him.

Chapter Nine

Brooklyn couldn't remember a time when her body felt as totally invigorated and on fire as it was at this very moment. Chase's warm, naked skin practically infused with hers, awakened a new awareness of being alive and enamored by a man. No, this wasn't her first time with a man, but it was the first time she'd experienced these emotions before thanks to Chase. Deep down, she wanted to erase the one night only suggestion; however, she knew it was for the best and promised herself to savor every second encased with him.

Flipping her over onto her stomach, he pushed his hand into her hair and trailed scorching kisses on her neck. His other hand roamed down her side and clenched her bottom, rotating it in a gentle, sensual motion.

"Mmm … Chase …" she barely managed to croak out as his kneading on her bottom sped up with each passing second and her hips automatically joined the same rhythm. "Oh, Chase …"

"Love hearing you say my name," he whispered against her ear as he continued grasping onto her.

His tongue left her neck and began to make an unhurried yet exaggerated path down her back. Grasping the pillow, Brooklyn's pulse sped up at the anticipation of where his tongue headed toward. The thought caused her to clutch the pillow harder and she hoped goose feathers weren't about to spill out and fly around them. Heat radiated through her body, enhanced by his lips on her skin, and the satisfied groans aroused from his throat tingled her center. Her moans increased as his tongue glided down, and she drew in a sharp breath when he abruptly stopped at the small of her back. She was almost disappointed when he slid his body up to rest on top of her. Chase glided his tongue along her neck until he reached it around to her lips, capturing her mouth and muffling the gasp which was about to erupt as he slid his hand way from her butt. Placing it between her thighs, he parted them wide and caressed her warm center in a circular motion, causing the hint of an orgasm to begin a slow rise.

"Mmm … mmm," she sighed out. "Damn, that feels …" Her voice trailed off as he delved his tongue deeper into her mouth.

"Thank you," he boasted, with his mouth lingering over hers, as he flipped her over, causing a resounding giggle from her. "Glad you're enjoying the sample."

"Sample?" she questioned as his mouth left hers and he captured a breast into his mouth. "Whew! Mmm … Chase," she breathed out as his teased the other one into his mouth.

"I'm just getting started," Chase said, staring up at her with dark eyes. "We have all night." He traveled his mouth back and forth between each breast, making sure to give both equal attention as if he couldn't decide which one he liked more.

"Um, I have an early morning flight," she reminded, not that she cared at the moment.

"Sleep on the plane, beautiful and dream of my tongue …" he paused, sliding it down the middle of her body until it reached between her thighs, and slowly licked the delicate little bud into his mouth, "here."

"Oh… Chase." Arching her head against the pillow, Brooklyn reached down to grasp his shoulders, but he placed her hands onto the bed and held them tight under his.

His tongue and mouth never missed a beat of the erotic dance he bestowed upon her over and over, causing one of her legs to shake uncontrollably. Brooklyn intertwined her fingers with his, and her hips met his tongue in the same tempo as the other leg began to shake. She wanted to beg him to replace his tongue with something else; however, the only word she could whisper out was, "Chase," as the soar of a climax began to rage, shaking her entire body. Grasping her hips, Chase didn't stop but instead slowed down to a sensual pace as her breathing calmed somewhat to normal and she let out a peaceful, long sigh.

"Mmm … that was exquisite," Brooklyn moaned.

She attempted to sit up to return the favor, but apparently Chase wasn't finished as his tongue sunk even deeper into her, followed by one of his fingers and another, sending Brooklyn once again on the roller coaster ride she thought she'd gotten off of. He was right. She would definitely be on the airplane daydreaming of this very act of rapture which had to be the next best thing to heaven. Blissful waves of elation crashed through her veins, and the effortless chore of breathing was no longer easy.

Brooklyn didn't know how long this go around of pure pleasure lasted and she barely remembered staring at him through her haze of ecstasy as he scooted off the bed and rustled around in his shorts that lay on the floor. She heard the rip of something before he rejoined her, gathered her in his arms, and placed his lips on hers in a slow-winding kiss. Wrapping her legs around his waist, her eyes pleaded with his to make them one. A sly smile inched across Chase's face while he slid one of his hands down between them to honor her silent request. Their lips joined at the same time, and were in sync together in an identical unhurried and sensual tempo.

A wave of tantalizing emotions ripped through her as he began to plunge deeper, causing her to shudder all over again; but unlike earlier, her orgasm was even more uncontrollable and she clutched his shoulders tight for the fear of falling because she no longer felt the mattress under her. Instead, she was floating on air in Chase's arms as he stroked in and out of her at a pace that sped up with each inch of thrusting, which she happily matched until he eventually could no longer hold on, and gripped her tight as he shuddered against her.

All of the daydreams, fantasies, and night dreams she'd ever had of making love with him didn't even come close to the way he was making her feel physically and emotionally. It didn't compare, and she didn't know how on Earth she wasn't going to crave him after tonight. She sensed withdrawals in her future from not being able to be touched or kissed by Chase, and he knew exactly what he was doing. Erasing away her proposition of one night only. It sure as hell was working, but she knew nothing more could come of their tryst, and she decided to savor the moment instead.

They made love one more time before taking a shower together and settling back in the bed naked and entangled in each other's arms, facing each other under the comforter.

"How many hours of sleep of do we have?" she asked groggily with a yawn.

"About three. I set my cellphone alarm. I'm deep sea fishing in a few hours you know."

"I'm sure you'll have fun," she said sleepily, her eyes dropping but she was still halfway coherent.

"Not as much fun as I had tonight," he yawned, closing his eyes.

Brooklyn nestled closer to him. "I knew our one night together would be magical."

"One night?" he asked just above a whispering chuckle on her forehead before pulling her closer against his comforting chest. "I'm never letting you go."

Brooklyn tried to pretend she didn't hear the words he uttered as she drifted off to sleep but she had. And they rang loud in her head throughout her dreams.

*****

Chase kissed the top of Brooklyn's forehead and slid out of the bed moments after his cellphone alarm sounded. Turning on the lamp, he grabbed his shorts from the antique storage chest in front of the bed and slipped them on. It was nearly five in the morning, and even though they had barely slept four hours, Brooklyn felt wide awake and recharged. A feeling of melancholy washed over her as their one night had come to an end. It had been everything she imagined and more, but she knew anything past this wouldn't be in her best interest as she was already in a complicated place in her life, and she didn't want to add to it.

"I hate to leave so early, but Addi sent a text to be ready at six for our deep sea fishing excursion, and she has a surprise for me later. I'm almost scared to find out. Knowing her it's swimming with the sharks or something else life threatening. Too bad you can't come."

Brooklyn crawled to the foot of the bed as he sat and put on his shoes. She knew of the surprise and it wasn't anything life threatening. He rustled her hair, and she was terrified to even glance in the mirror to witness how bad it looked. But she didn't care. It was worth it after being with him.

"Oh yeah," she stated with a slight chuckle, glancing at her packed suitcase by the door. She'd almost forgot about her trip home. "Gotta plane to catch."

"I'll miss you, but I can't wait until you come back so I can make love to you again." He paused, drawing her to him and kissing her deeply on the lips. "And again."

Fear shook through her at his words. Not that she didn't want to, but last night had been a one-time escapade. Did he forget? However, his statement of "I'm never letting you go," replayed in her head, and she knew he was serious.

The seductive expression on his face wasn't making what she didn't want to say any easier. She knew her decision would be for the best in the long run even though there was a dumbbell that weighed a ton lying on her chest and voices (Reagan and Zaria's) screaming in the back of her head, "Girl, are you crazy?"

Brooklyn tried to breathe out but couldn't. "I don't regret what happened," she quickly said as she witnessed his smile fade. "But we agreed to have this one night and it was amazing. Let's not ruin the moment with talks of something which will never be."

Sure enough his face scrunched into a ball of confusion and then turned into a grin followed by a light, sarcastic laugh. "Ha. I understand .And then next time we see each other you'll break your promise and give in to temptation once more?" His inquiry was laced with a slight condescending sneer.

"No, I don't think you do. I like you ...a lot, but your stay here is temporary. You're going back to Memphis in December, and honestly, right now I'm in limbo about my next career move. I have no idea where it's going to take me. I may stay here on St. Simons but not necessarily with Precious Moments, and I know I'm not moving back to Memphis and you're not moving here. I need to focus on me at the present. I've always helped others achieve their dreams, but I have yet to fulfill my own. Starting a new relationship at this moment wouldn't be wise. True, we can hang out and have fun and whatnot, but in the end you'll be leaving in a few months."

Groaning, he ran his hands over his face and backed away from her. "I truly understand how you feel, but I'm not trying to stand in the way of your career plans or dreams. Not trying to rush you into a relationship, but I honestly see a future with you. I can't lie about that."

"Chase, I think we got caught up in a fairy tale fantasy of each other because we've always been attracted to one another. We were curious about the possibilities."

"But who knows what may happen in the future?"

"I don't want to become so caught up with you or fall in love with you and then you leave. True, I can go to Memphis, but moving back there isn't in any part of my plans. I love to visit my brother and his family, but it hasn't felt like home since my parents died."

"So basically what you're saying is you don't want to continue seeing me on any level for the fear of falling for me … or you've already fallen for me and now you're scared?"

Okay, so he knows me better than I realized. "I think it's best we cool it …"

"Oh, now I see." He stood and stepped away from the bed. "When you say," he put his fingers up to symbolize quotation marks, "'it's *best we cool it*,' you mean wave hi and bye if we run into each other while I'm still at Addi's but not hang out alone because you're scared what it could lead to like last night for example."

Standing in front of him, she tried to hold back the tears. "Chase, I'm sorry. I think we should cut our losses now before we get too involved. You want something I can't give at the moment. I was serious when I said one night only."

"This sounds like one of those 'it's not you, it's me' type of speeches." He stepped into her personal space as her breath sucked in sharply. "And you know what? It is *you* because it's definitely not me. It's you. It's you scared of heartbreak. It's you not willing to give us a chance. It's you not having faith if we are meant to be everything will fall into place. It's you, because I know what I want." He grabbed her to him but he didn't kiss her. Instead, he stood still, his jaw clenched as his stare penetrated into her. "And you know what you want as well. It's been written on your beautiful face since the moment we met. It's in the way you kiss me, touch me. The way you look at me. The way we made love. It wasn't casual sex and you know it." He meshed her against him and whispered on her parted lips, "We breathe in sync."

Knowing all of what he stated was true, Brooklyn didn't have a comeback answer, but she wasn't going to change her mind. It was for the best even if it did hurt like pure hell.

"I'll respect your wishes, but we'll see how long it takes for you to change your mind ... again. And while I would love for you to do so, please know I'm not going to wait around forever, sweetheart." Chase chuckled nervously, released her, and strolled toward the bedroom door. "I don't ride roller coasters," he called out before shutting the door.

Brooklyn didn't know how long she stood with her feet rooted to the hardwood floor as the tears streamed down her face. After making sure her home was secure, she trekked back to her bedroom. Her mind continued to replay the conversation with Chase. Her motto of 'sometimes you have to do the right thing even when you don't want to' applied to this situation. Her head knew she made the right decision, but her heart was mad as hell and refused to beat correctly as it sped up followed by a crash sending her under the covers as the tears continued to flow well after she left for the airport wearing aviator shades.

Chapter Ten

"When you said you had a surprise for me after deep sea fishing, I'd feared it was something like base jumping off of the island's lighthouse," Chase stated to Addison as he hugged his twin brother, Hunter, and then picked up and spun around his other baby sister, Zoe. The twins focused on each other's outfits and realized they had on the same Yale Law school T-shirt and a pair of khaki shorts.

"Great minds," the twin brothers stated in unison followed by a series of daps, handshakes, and fists bumps they'd made up when they were children.

"I figured we needed a mini Arrington reunion," Addison said, intertwining her arm with Zoe's. "We've all been so busy and spread out this year."

"I agree," Hunter said. "We haven't hung out just the four us since Zoe passed the bar."

"Well, it's great to see you both." Chase was glad they were there. Perhaps he could rid his mind of Brooklyn and her antics with this welcomed distraction. "Now I know why Addi was adamant about cooking out today."

"The crew is all here," Zoe said as they sat down in redwood Adirondack chairs set in conversation-style in front of Addison's tiny house.

Grabbing their beer bottles from the table in the middle, the siblings toasted while waiting for the trout that Addison and Chase caught that morning to finish grilling along with corn on the cob, and sweet potatoes. Addison also made a big pot of spaghetti and meatballs the night before to go along with the fish, which was a family tradition most weekends when they were growing up.

"Still can't believe Addi talked you into staying here," Hunter started, nodding his head toward the tiny home. "How do you do it, bruh?"

"Man, it's not easy climbing into that loft. You two should bunk with us," Chase joked. "It will be like that one time our parents rented an RV for a cross-country trip for the summer."

Zoe laughed, swiping a lock of her hair from her pixie-cut off her forehead. "And after the second night, Mom demanded a hotel room. Only Addi enjoyed the RV, obviously. No, thank you. We'll stay in the condo we rented, but Addi's home is perfect for her," she added, squeezing her sister's hand. "We're all so proud."

"Those were good times, and even though it's out of my norm, at least I'm chilling with baby sis," Chase said. "I have enjoyed staying here."

He caught his siblings giving each other knowing glances as if they knew an inside joke. "What? I've enjoyed my time here." Standing, he went to check on the food, and had a sneaky inkling of what they were referring to. He knew them all well. Addison and Zoe told each other everything no matter what, and he'd mentioned to Hunter a few days ago he'd been hanging out with Brooklyn.

Zoe took a swallow of her beer and popped her lips. "Mmm-hmm. So we heard, loverboy."

"Did you finally convince her of a real date or is she still calling it hanging out?" Hunter asked, strolling to the grill and taking the corn on the cob off. "Even though you can't keep your hands off of each other."

"Yes, do tell," Addison chimed in. "You came in this morning right before we left for deep sea fishing."

Taking the trout off the grill, Chase placed them on a nearby platter and covered them with foil. "She decided she doesn't want any type of relationship." Shrugging, he plopped back in his seat and took a long swig of his beer. "She's scared of something. I don't know. I don't have time for wishy-washy."

"Long distance issues?" Hunter asked. "It was Harper's gripe early on in our relationship, but true love conquers all."

Chase shook his head in the negative. "No. It's not the eventual distance she's concerned about even though I think she's using it as an excuse. She's in some kind of career/life limbo at the moment and it's her main focus. Not sure if I believe that's the reason either."

"Well, she does have a great opportunity with Kameryn, and who knows what doors will open for her after this," Addison reminded. "Personally, who wants to be tied down to a man when there's so much more to the world besides being with someone who can't appreciate the value of ..." Addison ceased as her siblings eyed her with concerned expressions. Taking the last swig of her beer, she cleared her throat and shooed a lovebug which had landed on her hand away. "But you're a great guy to be tied down to, Chase. It's just not my cup of tea."

"Gee, thanks,' Chase said sarcastically. "She also mentioned Memphis no longer feels like home to her since her parents are deceased which I do understand. She's working through something, and I came along at the wrong time in her life, I guess."

"Ah, I see," Zoe said as an empathetic expression formed on her face. "Fortunately, we don't know the feeling. I can't imagine Mommy and Daddy not being here. Has to be hard. I'm sure Rasheed and Brooklyn were devastated when their parents died. It was just the two of them, and now Rasheed has his family. Perhaps Brooklyn feels alone in some aspects."

Hunter rejoined them and handed everyone another beer. "But don't give up. I knew Harper was the one for me even when she kept trying to push me away and make believe she wasn't in love with me, and now we're going to have triplets. Triplets," he chuckled nervously, taking a swig from the bottle. "I need something stronger than this beer."

"I still can't believe it," Zoe said as her and Addison got up to make their plates. "However, when the dad is a twin and the mom is a triplet, multiples can happen, you know."

"Apparently," Hunter said teasily with a clenched jaw. "We were shocked yet elated when the doctor said there were three heartbeats. Six more long months of waiting to see their adorable little faces in person and not on the sonogram screen."

"How's Harper feeling?" Chase asked, relieved the focus was off of him.

"Irritable and happy all at the same time. Oh, and very hungry along with being in decoration mode. She's begun gathering ideas for the nursery and childproofing the house, so I can only imagine what to expect when I return to Atlanta on Monday."

"I can't wait," Addison beamed, placing spaghetti on her paper plate. "The Arrington triplets. Sounds so cool. But back to you, Chase. I've witnessed you and Brook together. I haven't known her long, but I noticed a change in her when you arrived. She's usually serious and focused but lately she's been carefree. Kind of like you. Something has awakened both of your spirits. I do know she's been in a rut with work. She mentioned it to me over dinner one night, but she isn't ready to tell Reagan and Zaria. She's not happy with living the same routine over and over. Trust me, that can be boring which is why I don't do it.

Brook hasn't fully disclosed everything to me and her best friends, but I'm all for seeking one's inner desires. I wouldn't say you came along at the wrong time. Falling for someone has no wrong or right time. So don't give up. If it's meant to be, the two of you will find a way."

Chase noted the solemn tone hidden in her upbeat voice, and he had a feeling her mind was on her ex who had sent the flowers yesterday. Despite the fact she'd avoided discussing him like the black plague for the past couple of years, Chase and the entire family knew Addison still loved him but wasn't ready to forgive or settle in one place either.

"I'm not giving up. I'm an Arrington man." Chase and Hunter bumped their fists and clinked their beer bottles. "We want something, we see it through until the end."

Zoe pursed her lips and peered over her shades at the twin brothers. "Arrington women don't give up either, thank you." She bumped fists with Addison, followed by a finger snap in a half-circle. "Carry on."

Chase shook his head with a smirk at his sassy sister who reminded him of their mother. They both may be petite in stature and appear sweet … until it's necessary to unleash their wrath. His mother had been a beast in the courtroom and no doubt Zoe was following in her footsteps.

"I'm going to give Brooklyn some time. I know what it's like to be in a career limbo."

"Yeah, you should know," Zoe agreed, taking a bite of her fish. "Are you ready to join me at the firm? I need you, big brother, since these two knuckleheads are never coming." She cut her eyes jokingly at Addison and Hunter.

"I'll be there, and don't act like you're always there, Ms. Political Analyst," Chase said, knowing he was about to crawl under her skin. "Thanks to technology, I'm able to listen to you on *Good Morning, Memphis* on the way to work. You're bound to become a regular for the political segments."

"I can do both, along with teaching the bar exam prep class you used to teach, and still find time to volunteer at the women's shelter."

Chase wasn't surprised at his spitfire sister's answer. "I know, superwoman, but must you be so mean at times? I felt sorry for one of the men you told off last week, and you know I can't stand him either."

Hunter nodded his head in agreement. "I'm actually able to watch, and did you have to say 'bye, Felicia and miss me with the nonsense' along with the eye roll for a touch of dramatics?" he asked, cracking a smile.

She rolled her eyes sarcastically. "If he continues to tell lies about *my* president, then I'll continue telling him and the rest of them off," Zoe replied matter-of-factly.

"You know *your* president isn't the president anymore," Chase joked, knowing Zoe would probably curse him out next.

Zoe placed her plate on the table and stood with her hands proudly on her hips. "A) he will always be *my* president and B) if that man or any of the other political pundits continue to tell lies and half-truths, they will feel my wrath as I set them straight with the facts." Zoe smacked her lips. "Had the audacity to say the economy isn't where it is today because of our last president. Chile, don't get me started. I'm supposed to be on vacation."

Addison's cell phone ringing and subsequent grimace as she tossed it on the table and strolled to the ice chest caused the siblings to glance at each other with concern. Taking out a bottled water, she began to down it.

"Addi?" Zoe asked, quietly. "What's wrong?"

Addison mustered a fake smile. "Nothing ... I didn't recognize the number," she answered, reaching into the other ice chest and pulling out a bag of shrimp marinating in teriyaki sauce. "Finish telling us about the pundit you had to tell off while I grill these shrimp."

The phone rang once more and Addison stormed toward it. "Time to change the ring tone to 'Sorry' by

Beyonce or put your ass back on block." Glaring in anger at the screen, she exhaled in relief. "Oh, it's Brook. Hey, girl." She was silent for a moment while listening. "Sure. I'll go grab the keys to your house and handle it for you." More silence. "It's no problem. I'll call you back in a bit."

"Is she okay?" Chase asked, surprised at the concern which arose in his chest.

"She forgot something," Addison answered, disappearing into her house to retrieve the keys.

"Oh," Chase said with a simple nod as his thoughts trekked back to what he was hoping his siblings' visit would distract him from. However, he decided not to focus on it and instead tuned into more of Zoe's unapologetic rants from *Good Morning, Memphis* which set him into a hysterical laughing mode even if he didn't mean it.

*****

Thanks to over sleeping the alarm buzz after crying herself back to sleep after her decision to stop seeing Chase cold turkey, Brooklyn forgot to download the pictures from the museum shoot off of her desktop and onto a zip drive. Hearing Chase's laugh in the background when Addison called back set her heart speeding like a greyhound around a race track. He seemed happy and unbothered, which for some reason bothered the hell out of her. Not that she wanted him mopey and upset, but men had a way of moving on and forgetting while she couldn't count the number of sleepless nights she'd had over a relationship not working out.

After checking the email Addi sent and replying back with a sincere thank you, Brooklyn rejoined Rasheed and Bria on their walk on Beale Street in downtown Memphis. They'd finished an early dinner at Lillian's Dinner and Blues Club which was owned by Reagan's brother, Justin Richardson, who was also the executive chef, along with his best friend, Derek Martin, who was the general manager. Rasheed had once been a part owner, and

Brooklyn even was a hostess for a spell after college before landing a job at an accounting firm.

"Everything all right now, sis?" Rasheed asked. His warm, cinnamon-colored eyes that matched their late father's bore into her as if he was expecting a negative answer.

"Yep. Can't believe I forgot something so important." Brooklyn had purposely placed Bria in the middle to avoid any eye connection with her brother. But considering he was over six foot five and his wife was barely five foot six in heels, the idea hadn't work.

"Yeah, not like you. You seem off today. What's up?"

"Nothing." She shrugged, skipping her heels over a grate on the sidewalk as Chase's laugh still filled her head. She'd laughed all through dinner as well, but hers hadn't been genuine as she used it to mask the hurt she caused herself.

"You almost missed your flight this morning," Rasheed reminded. "Not like you either."

"Rasheed, stop," Bria interjected, rubbing Brooklyn's back and taking her husband's newsboy cap off and playfully hitting his bald head with it. "Everyone is entitled to an off day."

"I know," Rasheed said, squeezing his wife's hand. "I'm a concerned big brother, Bree."

"Well, we are both excited about the book with Kameryn Monroe," Bria said in a comforting manner, tossing a leave-Brooklyn-alone expression to her husband. "She's so talented, and the exhibit at the Memphis Botanical Gardens is exquisite. Traci invited the entire family to the private showing. It's good to be related to one of the head botanists at the gardens."

Brooklyn was grateful of Bria's change of subject. "I saw some of the displays on the garden's website and fell in love. I can only imagine how they'll appear in person. I spoke to Traci briefly yesterday to go over last minute details. She sounded exhausted."

"Well, between you and me, I think her and my brother are expecting, but it may be too early for them announce. He's been giddy lately and Sean Arrington is never giddy about anything," Bria informed them with a bright smile showcasing deep dimples.

"Aww … babies are so precious," Brooklyn gushed. "It's wonderful if true. They'll make great parents."

"They will, and I just found out my cousin, Hunter, and his wife, Harper, are having triplets."

"Wow. Triplets! That's a lot of diapers," Brooklyn laughed, even though the mention of Hunter made her think about his twin brother. She knew Addison was going to surprise him with a visit from their siblings, and from the sounds of laughter in the background during their phone call it seemed like they were all having a blast.

"Yeah, twins run in the Arrington-Chase families, but this will be the first set of triplets thanks to Harper who is the youngest of triplets. Anyway, Rasheed and I are so happy you're here. We hate months going by before we see you. I know you love St. Simons but don't forget about family and home."

Home? Brooklyn held in a sentimental sigh. Nowhere felt like home at the moment. She didn't want to tell Rasheed and his wife because Memphis was their home, but they had each other. The majority of Bria's immediate family lived there and they'd welcome Rasheed with open arms. When Brooklyn graduated from college she felt alone. Rasheed was in and out of town with *Sports Fanatic* as the show's lead basketball analyst, and while she had Reagan and Zaria, there was still a hole in her heart she knew would never mend. Being in Memphis only reminded her of it. However, she needed to brush all of it to the side, including the thoughts of Chase which continued to creep into her being as well. She had begun to silently chastise herself as she second-guessed the decision to end it with him before things grew too complicated. Even though she supposed sleeping with him definitely added onto complicating the situation. However, Brooklyn was shocked she'd admitted to him about Memphis no longer feeling like home because of her parents; though, she was also homesick at times which left her in a frustrated, contradictory mood.

They turned on Main Street and stopped in a front of a two-story building with a for sale sign in the window. She remembered the different businesses and its interior well. It used to be a spa owned by a high school friend of hers, and before that a photography studio owned by Ms. Tate a family friend who'd mentored Brooklyn when she began to show interest in photography. It was a gesture she'd always been grateful for, and it prompted her to do the same throughout the years with budding photographers.

"When did Shaunie close her spa?" she asked, trying to peek through the cracks of the boarded up windows. The space was open, as if the walls were all torn down. She glanced at the sign which stated the area was three thousand square feet with an additional one thousand square feet of living area of upstairs.

"Earlier this year," Rasheed answered. "Your old friend got married and moved to Atlanta. This place has been for sale for months."

"I remember when we used to come here for our childhood pictures because Mom never liked the school pictures' plain backgrounds. She wanted something more elaborate yet personal."

"Yeah, that's where you get your creative side from. Always thinking outside of the box."

"Remember the time we posed with Bonnie, our rabbit?" Brooklyn asked, reminiscing about the Easter when she was eight years old and her parents had given her a pet rabbit. "I still have the picture in a frame. You were fly in your pastel blue suit," she teased, knowing her brother hated the three-piece suit their mother thought he looked adorable in.

Rasheed stepped next to his sister and squeezed her hand. "Mom wanted everything to be perfect."

"Because she is … was perfect." Brooklyn's voice cracked as Rasheed placed his arm around her shoulders, pulling her close to him.

"Yes, she is, baby sis. I miss her every day. Dad as well."

"Me too." She swiped away a tear that formed in the corner of her eye.

"We can go put flowers on their graves before you leave like we always do when you come home."

"I'd love to go."

"Great. Let me know if you can steal away from the shoot at the garden tomorrow."

"Of course."

"Now. Our next stop before heading home is …" Rasheed's lips broke into a wide smile across his face and his eyebrows perked up waiting for her answer.

"It better be Ollie's Sweets," she exclaimed, grabbing Bria and Rasheed's hands and pulling them toward the trolley which had stopped a few feet in front of them. "A huge slice of her Memphis Mud Pie is what I need before tomorrow's long day." Brooklyn glanced back at the vacant building one last time as she stepped onto the trolley.

Chapter Eleven

Brooklyn tapped her fingers on the kitchen counter next to the stove as she contemplated zooming out onto the patio like the DC Comic's character The Flash to snip a few sprigs of rosemary and basil for the cavity of the chicken she was preparing to roast. However, she'd noticed Chase's BMW drive up moments before, and she'd caught him scurrying into the tiny house with a take-out bag. She returned late last night from Memphis and hadn't had the daunting pleasure to run into him. Brooklyn hoped they wouldn't have an encounter for the rest of the week until he would be on his merry way to Jacksonville for the remainder of the semester. A piercing jolt pinched her heart every time she thought about him during what little free time she had when she was out of town. The session lasted for two days thanks to unexpected thunderstorms which placed a damper on capturing photos of the glass art flowers that were mostly outside in the garden areas. Brooklyn was also disappointed for not being able to visit her parents' gravesite before leaving Memphis.

Sighing, she grabbed the kitchen shears from the knife holder and headed toward the backdoor.

This will only take a moment. Besides, he's inside eating his food.

Upon opening the door, she spotted Chase sitting in one of the red Adirondack chairs outside of the tiny house. Their eyes caught each other's in an instant and stayed captured like a fly in a sticky spider web. He'd been in the process of taking a swig of his water and the bottle stayed midair before he placed it in the cup holder of the chair.

A smidge of a smirk displayed on his face. "Hi," he said after a few moments of the uneasy silence. "How was Memphis?"

Okay. He's being cordial even though the smug expression says he's definitely upset with me. Brushing her hair back behind her ears, Brooklyn tried to shut down the stammer rising in her throat. "Good. It was cool seeing my family, and of course the botanical garden shoot." *Okay, that wasn't so bad. Now clip the dang herbs and go back inside. Oh wait, my feet are glued to the patio.* "How was the surprise visit with Zoe and Hunter?"

"It was great catching up with them. Made me homesick for Memphis, though, but I'll be back there soon."

More uneasy silence filled the atmosphere as she remembered his leaving soon was one of the reasons she felt there was no point in starting a serious relationship with him.

"Were you able to see Addison before she left?" he asked, swirling his fork around in the take-out box with a slight grimace.

"Yes. I took her to pick up the RV van this morning. It was very nice inside. Cute little kitchen, a full bathroom, seating area, and a Murphy bed. Flat screen." *Why am I rambling? Clip the damn herbs and go!*

"I know she'll enjoy herself … well, except for seeing Langston Graham."

Brooklyn shook her head in puzzlement at the name. "Wait, not the professional golfer …"

"Yep, he's her ex. *The ex.*"

That explains the flowers, ignored phone calls, and text messages, Brooklyn thought. "Oh ... he'll be there?"

"The groom is his cousin so more than likely."

"Bless her heart. Now I know why she's been on edge lately. Running into someone who you used to date can be uncomfortable if it didn't end on good terms."

He raised an arrogant eyebrow along with a swished-to-the-side grin. "Yep, it sure can be," Chase said sarcastically.

"Insert foot in mouth right now. I'm so sorry."

"No need to apologize." He lightly shrugged. "I mean, we weren't a couple like them, but we've known each other just as long, and I thought we were finally taking a step to another level. You know ... something I thought we'd both wanted not a one-night stand."

"I just—"

"Stop." He held up his hand in a halting gesture. "You don't need to explain anything to me." He paused, glancing at the scissors in her hand.

Feeling as if it was a silent reminder as to why she was out there in the first place and his way of ending the conversation, Brooklyn walked over to the herb stand where eight flower pots contained different herbs. She clipped a few sprigs of what she needed and headed back in the house without glancing his way even though she felt his stare singeing her back the entire time.

After cleaning the kitchen from the chicken, mashed sweet potatoes, and collard green dinner she barely ate, a flicker of light caught her attention from the back window of the keeping room. The sun had set moments ago and Addison's timed lights would automatically turn on above the porch along with the two spotlights resting in each top corner of her tiny home. However, they were noticeably not on and a light continued to move back and forth. Brooklyn peeped through the shutter blinds and noticed Chase outside again. This time he was tinkering with the solar generator on the side of Addison's home. The panel door was open as he knelt in front of it using his cellphone as a flashlight.

Sighing, Brooklyn headed to the kitchen junk drawer, grabbed the flashlight, flicked it on to make sure the batteries worked before she strolled along the paved path from her patio to the tiny house.

"I believe it has a reset button," she said in a quiet manner, while Chase looked up in surprise as she handed him the flashlight. The thought of resetting their relationship crossed her mind as soon as she said it. "It's happened before. You're running too many … electrical things at the same time … perhaps." Brooklyn silently scolded herself for stumbling over her words in front of him. She'd decided to assist on an impulse and now the same smug expression he wore earlier caused her to regret the decision to help.

Standing, he wiped the beads of sweat from his forehead. "Yeah. I called Addi and she said the same but it isn't turning back on. Maybe a blown fuse or something. I don't know. She said it's never done this before and what's in storage is almost gone."

"Oh, no. She upgraded to this generator and solar panels at the beginning of the summer."

"It's still under warranty, and I have the number to call in the morning. Hopefully they can come out soon," he said, his tone laced with agitation.

"Let me know, and I can be here just in case you're in class," she offered. "I'll be in my home studio most of the day finishing up some projects."

"No," Chase said without hesitation, "I got it."

She didn't believe him as frustration tensed his usually calm features. But she had an inkling his frustration wasn't focused on the generator anymore.

"Thank you." Handing her the flashlight, he closed the panel and glanced at the time on his cellphone. "Anyway, I need to finish grading research papers that my students emailed me and my laptop's battery is on fifty percent." He took a step backwards as if he was going to leave.

"Well, you can sit at my kitchen table if you need to and bring whatever is in the fridge over that may spoil."

"I'm good, but thank you. It's only a few more papers. However, I will bring the fish over from the freezer, though. Addison would be pissed if it went bad."

Brooklyn was somewhat taken aback by his refusal, but she understood. "Chase … I know you're upset with me, but you have work to do and your laptop will be dead soon."

"I'm not upset with you."

"But you're trying to avoid me."

"Isn't that what you wanted?" he questioned. His tone rose into a deep baritone and this time his full attention was on her as he stepped into her personal space. "Giving you what you want, sweetheart."

Luckily, the two houses on either side of her were vacation rentals and were currently empty because she was sure his sarcastic statement was heard past her property.

Deep down, no. It's not what I want at all. Brooklyn couldn't tell him she regretted the moment she suggested they stop seeing each other. He was standing too close as if he was purposely tempting her with his seductive stare and a slight lick of his bottom lip as she rested her gaze on it for a moment. A sly fox grin slid across his face as if he knew she would take the bait he'd casted out.

Brooklyn smacked her mouth with a slight eye roll. "Whatever," she answered, turning on her heel toward her home. "I'll make room in the freezer for Addison's fish."

"Brooklyn, wait," he called out, sliding his hand around her arm in a soft grip.

She yanked her head sharply over her shoulder. "What?" she questioned, her tone transformed to a curt one but only to hide the regret rising in her chest and to extinguish the tears needing to fall. "Changed your mind about bringing the fish, too?"

"Wow," he said with a taken aback scoff. "No, I was going to say I'll take you up on your offer so I can finish grading the papers, but now you're the one with the attitude. I swear it should be the other way around."

"I don't have an attitude," she stated through clenched teeth. "And you've been quite smug, mister."

"You're the one wanting to end things before they even began which I respect, but why are *you* so frustrated over it?" he asked as sarcasm filled his tone.

"I'm not," she replied in a calm manner. "You're the one being all nonchalant and can barely look at me. I'm going off your vibe."

Sighing, he ran a hand over his bald head. "You know what? I was simply doing as you asked before you left. It's hard because the woman I want is less than two-hundred feet away from me and acts like she doesn't know what she wants when in actuality she knows exactly what she wants. It's in every single action you've taken."

"I'm sorry, Chase. I thought it would be better that way so we … so *I* wouldn't keep changing my mind and having the urge to … kiss you … or something every time I see you." *Of course it hasn't helped. He's sexy as hell when he's mad.*

"The *something* was quite amazing."

They both laughed, and for a moment it was if they were back to normal, but she had to maintain her distance.

"I'm sorry for being snappy. Bring the fish and the laptop when you're ready."

"And I'm sorry as well. I'll see you in a few moments, but only to bring the fish. I think the laptop has enough battery for the five or six papers I have left."

"No problem."

"Besides, if you're in my presence for too long, you may decide to act on whatever you're thinking at this moment." Winking, he pivoted on his heel and headed inside.

Sighing, Brooklyn knew he was right and wasn't sure how much longer she could hold out. It had been on the tip of her tongue to invite him to stay with her until the generator was fixed but she knew that would be pure torture.

*****

Brooklyn sat at the table on her patio the next afternoon while the repairman from the solar company accessed the issue with the generator. Addison had called her earlier in the day to see if she was available during the given time window. While Chase stated he didn't need her help, Brooklyn wasn't doing it for him but for her friend so it would be fixed before she returned from Hamilton Island.

She had a stack of photography magazines on the table to keep her busy, but her thoughts kept swinging back to last night. She hated Chase could see right through her, and he seemed determined to change her mind. Deep down, she'd almost wanted him to. In the period of time they'd spent together, her attraction for him sprouted into more. A part of her wanted to say forget the nonsense of being scared and enjoy his company while he's here, have a short fling and keep living life after he left. However, her heart contracted every time she thought of the idea because she would be miserable once he moved back to Memphis. She'd had harmless flings in the past and a couple of friends-with-benefits relationships, but they never transpired into anything real and it never bothered her. That's not what she wanted with Chase, and from his words and actions that's not what he wanted either. But she didn't see how they could have a meaningful relationship once he left.

When he returned with the fish last night, she busied herself by chatting on the phone with Reagan about an upcoming winter wedding. He'd mouthed thank you and quickly left even though deep down she wanted him to stay. The temptation to be in his arms and feel his passionate kisses on her body scorched every inch on her body. She didn't know how she was going to survive with him living directly behind her without crashing through the door and saying ignore everything I said. Of course if last night's insomnia persisted thanks to him, she'd never fall asleep. At the moment, she desired a much-needed nap as she felt and appeared like an extra in a zombie movie.

"Ms. Vincent?" The repairman approached, pushing his hands into his hunter green slacks.

Brooklyn glanced up from the unread page of the magazine with a slight jump. She forgot she wasn't alone. "Yes?"

"Well, I have good news and bad news. It can be repaired, but I'll have to order the part. It may take a few days to arrive. I'll call Ms. Arrington and let her know. Hopefully, I can come back this weekend."

"Wonderful. I'll contact her as well."

Moments after he left, Brooklyn heard the click of Chase's dress shoes on the pathway. She'd finished texting Addison who was relieved the generator could be fixed.

"Hey. Did I miss the repairman?" Chase asked, standing at the edge of the patio dressed impeccably in a blue suit. "I got stuck in traffic."

"Yeah. You just missed him. He has to order the part. He'll be back this weekend."

"Oh, mmm-hmm. I see …" His faced tensed for a moment as he tapped his chin in contemplation. "The storage is completely empty now." He spoke out loud but it seemed more so to himself as he took off his suit jacket.

"I guess you're finally going to a hotel," Brooklyn stated with pep in her tone, and the little sigh of relief had tried not to escape. Maybe now she wouldn't toss and turn at night knowing he was a few feet away from her. Perhaps she could stop brooding over whatever the hell they'd had and move on.

His eyebrows shot up like antennas. "Nah." A mischievous grin spread across his face like smooth butter. "I'll stay here."

Wait. What did he just say? "Um … there's no electricity, which means there's no AC."

"I opened the window last night, and I was fine. Plus, the cold water works."

"It was also cool last night which isn't always the case during this time of year. It rarely gets cold here." Standing, she swiped her magazines and cellphone from the table. "Suit yourself." She walked toward the door but turned her head around with a sly smile. "If you get hot and bothered … just knock."

Chase chuckled. "I should be saying the same to you."

"Oh, please. You being behind me is no bother, but if you want to sweat like a pig going to a Hawaiian luau for the next week have fun. Hope you've stocked up on deodorant and you can borrow my ice chest."

"Ah, so you don't mind me being *behind* you? *Again?* Good to know."

Screaming silently, Brooklyn cleared her throat and erased the image implanted in her brain of them in that sexual position. "I meant the fact the tiny house is in my back …You know what? I don't have to explain myself to you. I'm going inside my nice air conditioned home. Good evening." Twisting the door knob and stepping inside, she heard the same infectious laughter which had attracted her to him in the first place. Grinding her teeth, she shut the door along with his laugh, but she could still hear it ringing in her ears as she lay in bed later on that night once more in a state of insomnia.

Chapter Twelve

"Brooklyn, you're a life saver. Thank you so much for squeezing me into your busy schedule for my engagement pictures," Reagan said, perusing the proofs from her and Blake's photo session that morning on the beach. "We still don't have a wedding date, but we're narrowing it down to sometime in the spring. Still trying to decide if I want it here or in Memphis. I'm leaning toward Memphis but the weather is so wedding perfect here. I don't know ..." Reagan contemplated, ending on a sigh.

Zaria made a popping sound with her lips and took a swig of her water bottle. "Well, let us know as soon as you know so Brook and I can start planning your shower and bachelorette parties."

Reagan laughed and continued clicking through the pictures on Brooklyn's laptop as the ladies gathered outside on her patio sipping peach margaritas and eating Reagan's homemade guacamole with pita chips. There was a cool evening breeze from the Atlantic Ocean located a few blocks over. Brooklyn didn't want to sit outside for the fear of seeing Chase, but Zaria had stated she needed some fresh air. For the past two days, Brooklyn tried to avoid him, but somehow he'd managed to see her coming and going. He would wave or wink with a naughty gaze, knowing it sent her blood rushing through her veins at autobahn speeds. The only reason why she felt somewhat safe at the moment was because Blake and Garrett had invited Chase to play pool that evening while their wives hung out with her. The men had hit it off at the deep sea fishing excursion, and she was relieved he wasn't home. She still couldn't believe he stayed in the tiny house to annoy her. The temperature had to be uncomfortable. She'd spotted him yesterday in his car talking on the phone with the motor running and no doubt with the air conditioner blasting. He'd stayed in there for at least an hour eating and making phone calls until the sun went down.

"I love all of them," Reagan said. "I can't decide which ones to use, but I'll decide by tomorrow. I know you have a ton of projects before heading to Destin with Kameryn so I appreciate it."

"No problem, hon," Brooklyn answered as upbeat as possible, swirling a pita chip lazily in the guacamole. She'd been so deep in her thoughts she'd almost forgot her girls were there. "That's what best friends … are … for." She tried to suppress a yawn, but it came out regardless as she covered her mouth. "Destin isn't for another month or so …" She trailed off into another yawn.

Reagan shut the laptop lid. "Brook, stop it. You are obviously overworking yourself because you can't stop yawning. This morning you drank a whole pot of coffee at the shoot. Not a cup but the entire pot!"

"Maybe you need a break," Zaria suggested, gliding a chip around in the guacamole, but she placed it on the plate and opted for a plain pita chip instead.

"You sure you don't want any of the margarita?" Brooklyn asked Zaria who'd been quiet. "It's Addison's special recipe."

"No, I had spin class tonight and need to hydrate," Zaria snapped, taking another deep drink of her water.

"And stop trying to sway the subject elsewhere. What's up with you? You need a vacay from work? That's not an issue if that's the case."

Brooklyn sighed. "It's not work ... something else."

"What?" Reagan and Zaria asked in unison.

"Don't worry about it. You two have a lot going on in your own lives right now," Brooklyn answered as she had a sneaky feeling Zaria was pregnant. Addi had mentioned she caught Zaria vomiting over the side of the boat when they'd gone deep sea fishing, and Zaria had turned down champagne at Reagan's engagement party. She never turned down champagne.

"Excuse me?" Reagan questioned. "We're your friends. No, scratch that. We're sisters. Does this have something to do with your decision to stop seeing Chase cold-turkey?"

Letting out a deep breath, Brooklyn took a long sip of her margarita. "I haven't slept a wink knowing he's living in my backyard, and I can't go over there to extinguish all of my pent-up frustrations even though that's exactly what he wants," she rambled, exhaling. "He finds it utterly funny I'm frustrated."

"Then go extinguish the fire," Zaria suggested in her usual sassy tone. "That way you won't beat yourself up about it once he leaves with a bunch of what ifs."

"Um ... I did ... right before I left for Memphis and it was amazing. It was more than I expected, but everything I knew it would be."

Zaria and Reagan gasped at the same time as their eyes widened into saucers and glanced at each other in disbelief.

"I know. I know. It's not like me, but I had to have him. And now I'm having withdrawals big time."

"Who says it has to be a one-night stand?" Zaria inquired.

"Exactly," Reagan said, nodding her head in agreement. "When Addison told us he would be here for a few months, I knew it would be the perfect opportunity for the two of you to explore your attraction. He couldn't take his eyes off of you at my engagement celebration."

"So what's the issue?" Zaria demanded, pursing her lips while waiting for an answer.

"He only has a couple of months here before he goes back to Memphis. I don't want to become serious with him, and then can only see him every so often or never again. It doesn't matter." She shrugged followed by a heavy groan. "I've made my mind up. I'm not going to worry about it anymore." *Or at least not out loud.*

"So why not have fun while he's here?" Zaria asked, finishing her water. "You two are consenting adults."

Brooklyn dipped a pita chip in the guacamole and swirled it around, keeping her eyes downcast. "It's not easy."

"I can't believe we're having this conversation. You've been in love with the man since forever and you dumped him," Reagan said in disbelief. "You had a chance with him and you dumped him!"

"I didn't dump Chase. You have to be a couple for that, and I'm not in love with him."

"You keep telling yourself that. I was there when you first laid eyes on him." Reagan reached across the table and squeezed Brooklyn's hand followed by Zaria. "So what's the real deal? I know you well enough you're using distance as an excuse. What did he do to make you want to stop seeing him? Is he a male chauvinist or something?"

"No. He's a sweetheart. A true gentleman."

"Does he stink?" Zaria asked with a teasing grin.

Brooklyn playfully smacked Zaria's hand. "Girl, no. He smells divine."

"Well, I say hang out and if it becomes serious to the point of marriage, you can always move back to Memphis."

Brooklyn's forehead wrinkled as she was rather surprised Reagan said that. "I would have to leave Precious Moments."

"I know, and we'd miss you terribly, but I never thought you'd stay here forever with me and Zaria. It was more so our dream and you tagged along to help out, but you have so much more talent besides wedding photography. Kameryn obviously thinks so as well. Nothing wrong with spreading your wings, my sister," Reagan encouraged with a sincere smile.

"Exactly." Zaria nodded in agreement. "I feel the same way. You have your own calling and aspirations."

"Wow. I'm glad you two feel this way because lately I've been in a rut. I love working with Precious Moments, but you're right, I do eventually want to do other types of photography kind of like how I used to before I moved here when it was more of a side hobby from crunching numbers all day. Perhaps have my own studio." Her mind trailed back to the empty building in downtown Memphis.

"Ah. I knew something had been bothering you and it wasn't only Chase. I'm a little peeved you didn't tell us, though. Helloooooo ..." Reagan snapped her fingers playfully in the air. "We're your sisters for life."

"I know," Brooklyn answered, quietly. "I've wanted to discuss it with you for the past year or so but I wasn't sure how you'd take it."

Zaria scooted her chair back from the table. "Girl, this is your life and you have to live it how you see fit whether it's pertaining to your career or relationships. If eventually leaving Precious Moments or being with Chase makes you happy, I say go for it." Standing, she headed toward the patio door. "Too much water. I'll be back," Zaria said, dipping inside the house.

"Thank you. It's a relief to finally let it out. I'm not going to up and leave you high and dry without an in-house photographer or an accountant. I don't even know what my next step is. I'm glad I finally felt comfortable telling you guys everything that has been in my head lately."

"Well, whenever you're ready, we'll be fine. There are other photographers on the island and surrounding areas we've used before when we had more than one event, and your intern is pretty good. I've noticed you've been training her alot more lately. Now I know why. Sooooo, what about Mr. Arring—" Reagan halted while her eyes reached passed Brooklyn as footsteps sounded along the sidewalk and she began to wave. "Hi, guys. How was your game of pool?" she asked as Blake, Garrett, and Chase approached the table.

Blake kissed Reagan on the cheek. "I lost the bet, sweetheart."

"I hope it wasn't too much. We are planning a wedding you know," Reagan teased, and rubbed her nose against his.

"I think we'll be all right," Blake said, kissing Reagan softly on the lips.

"Where's Z?" Garrett asked.

"She ran to the ladies' room," Brooklyn answered, who'd noticed lately Garrett had been even more doting to Zaria than he already was.

"Ah, of course," Garrett stated as if he wasn't surprised. His gaze shifted to her empty seat with her tote bag hanging from the back of the chair and two empty bottles of water sat on the table in front of it. "She had spin class today." He took the empty water bottles and barely touched guacamole and tossed it in the garbage can off to the side.

Zaria returned moments later and gave her husband a hug and a kiss on the cheek. "Hey, G. Ready to go?"

"Yep. I know you've had a long day, Z." He grabbed her tote bag as Zaria hugged Brooklyn and Reagan.

"Ready, babe?" Blake asked, pulling out Reagan's chair.

"Yes." Reagan hugged Brooklyn. "All right, girl. Remember what we talked about and thanks again for the engagement pictures. I'll let you know which ones we want printed soon."

"No problem," Brooklyn answered, hoping Chase would leave as well. The strong scent of his cologne she remembered all too well penetrated her atmosphere.

After he said his good-byes to everyone, Chase crashed into the chair across from her and fiddled around on his cellphone for the next few seconds which seemed like an eternity.

"So, apparently you're good at pool," Brooklyn said, breaking the awkward silence and taking the last sip of her margarita. She almost reached for the pitcher to refill her glass but decided another one wouldn't be wise around him.

"Yeah. My grandfather taught me how to play when I was a little boy," he answered, setting his phone down. "It's a family thing. Hunter and I are always teaming up against Zoe and Addi. I have a pool table back home collecting dust. Do you play?"

"My brother tried to teach me, but it isn't my thing, I guess."

"I could teach you, but that would mean we'd have to spend time together."

"Do you want some of Reagan's infamous guacamole?" she offered, ignoring his comment. "Or a margarita?"

"No. I ate at the pool hall."

"Oh."

He cracked a wise-grin. "Trying to make me stay?"

"I'm being courteous to my friend's big brother while she's out of town."

"Ha! I mean more to you than your friend's big brother. I know you still reminisce about our special night."

"Please, you weren't all that." *Okay, I'm lying. The withdrawal shakes will soon emerge if he doesn't leave.*

Standing, he swiped his cellphone from the table and placed it on the holster clipped to his pants. He didn't move, but instead rested his eyes on her and shoved his hands in his pockets as if he didn't want to leave. "Good night, and sleep well. I'm less than a few feet away if you need *anything*." He turned on his heel and headed over to the tiny house before shouting over his shoulder, "Anything."

"I'm fine. Good night." She wanted to call after him considering Zaria and Reagan had given her the courage to see where her relationship with Chase could lead. Instead, she gathered the empty dishes from the patio table and darted inside to a cold shower before she acted on her desires.

Chapter Thirteen

Wiping his brow, Chase downed a cool bottle of water after his cold shower. He didn't know what the hell he was thinking when he'd decided to stay in the tiny house without any electricity. He knew it was possible because his sister called it dry camping minus the fact there was running water. However, if it wasn't for Brooklyn he would've hightailed it to a hotel. He'd come to the conclusion seeing her was more important than feeling comfortable. This was the first time he'd gone through these types of extremes, but Brooklyn created a jolt of power whenever she was near.

The thought of being away from her tore through his heart like a knife. He literally couldn't wait until the second his office hours ended in the afternoon to rush back to the island for a glimpse of her. He loved how she would huff or dart her eyes away from him when he'd waved or say hello, and it was worth staying there to drive her crazy.

Swiping his car keys and cellphone from the kitchen counter, Chase strode to the door with anticipation for the car's air conditioner and a burger from Brogen's. He spotted the lady who had been in his thoughts non-stop watering her patio herb garden with a watering can. She hadn't noticed him and seemed deep in thought. His eyes slid over her cut-off jean shorts hugging her hips and ample butt causing him to reminisce clutching the same part of her anatomy the night they made love.

Shifting slightly on his heel, he tried to push out the thoughts of making love to Brooklyn but it was becoming increasingly hard to do. He'd never had withdrawals from a woman before which rocked him to his core. Thanks to his vivid memories, he could see through her clothes as if he was Superman with X-ray vision. The T-shirt depicting Dorothy Dandridge as Carmen Jones did nothing to hide Brooklyn's supple breasts, the indent and curves of her waist, and her cute belly button with the beauty mark off to the left of it. Chase had to halt his thinking process as his eyes once again settled on her hips. The urge to grip them and pull her onto to him caused a strain against his pants.

She still hadn't noticed his presence, and while he could stare at her all day, Chase decided to clear his throat and speak.

"Hey," he called out, stopping directly in front of the patio.

Brooklyn jumped slightly and pivoted in his direction. Her eyes darted straight to his and a little breath escaped from her lips. "Oh, hi." Brooklyn swiped her hand through her hair. "I didn't hear you approach."

"I can tell. Everything all right?"

"Yes." Her gaze dashed from him and she continued to water the herbs, keeping her eyes away from his.

Chase had an inkling she wasn't telling the truth but decided not to press the issue. She was already on guard with him. "I'm headed to Brogen's. You want me to bring something back? Or you can come with me."

She glanced up momentarily. "No and no," she replied in a frustrated tone.

"Are you sure you're okay?" he asked concerned. It was one thing to joke with her, but he didn't want to make her upset.

"I have a lot on my mind lately, and I'm thinking it through before making a rushed decision. *Again.*"

He sensed her uneasiness and decided to speak as light-hearted as possible. "About us?" he asked, stepping onto the patio. "Or work-related?" Either way, he was willing to offer an ear to listen.

She set the watering can on the table and advanced toward him but fell short of his personal space and took a step back. "Us, but I'm not sure how to tell you because you don't do roller coasters, and I don't want you to think I'm wishy-washy … I can admit I've been that way with you and I'm sorry. I'm usually not so indecisive and I hate it."

"Ah, I see."

"Do you?" she asked quietly.

"Yes," he answered with sincerity. "You're at a crossroads in your life and you don't want to make any bad decisions or mistakes. I can promise you being with me won't be a mistake. The other night wasn't a fling to me, and I know it wasn't for you no matter how you to try to proclaim it was a one-night stand. If I didn't think there was something between us, I wouldn't be 'dry camping' for the next few days in my sister's tiny house. I would've bounced already from it and out of your life."

"Chase, I would love to hang with you and whatnot while you're here, but no strings attached and no pressure from you to want more once you go back to Memphis. I can't promise anything after you leave. It's not a long distance issue per say, because I'm not moving back to Memphis so there's no reason to continue a relationship when you leave. But I don't want to feel pressured."

"I didn't realize I was pressuring you. I'm sorry. When I look at you I see more than right now. I see a future. I have to admit that scares me a bit for I can't remember a time I've thought about a woman in this way, and I wanted to explore more with you. However, we'll do it your way." *For now,* he added in his head.

"Thank you. I appreciate it. I mean, who says two grown people can't be carefree and live in the now?"

"Exactly." *But you're still not getting away from me that easy,* he thought.

She glanced passed him and stepped into his personal space. "You don't have to stay in the hot, tiny house or the rental. Stay with me. We'll have fun and not worry about anything else." She reached out her hand to shake his. "We have a deal?"

A smirk crossed his face at her held-out hand. "This isn't a business arrangement, sweetheart." Pulling Brooklyn to him, he dipped her and kissed her deeply on the lips. "This is a much better way to seal the deal." Chase lifted her back up but didn't loosen his grip from her hips. His hands were relieved to be right where they were and his heart felt the same way.

She slipped out of his embrace but clutched onto to his hand, leading him through the backdoor of her home. "I can think of another one." She winked. "And then afterwards, burgers!"

"Sounds like the perfect plan," Chase said, gathering her in his arms and walking toward her bedroom. "You will definitely need some fuel in between sessions."

Brooklyn laughed hysterically until he laid her down on the bed and kissed her with all the vigor pent up inside of him. Chase honestly couldn't believe he agreed to this arrangement, but he knew in his heart they were meant to be since the moment they'd met. And he wasn't giving up.

*****

"You're in great spirits," Reagan stated to Brooklyn as they perused a rack of sample bridesmaids' gowns in a bridal boutique in downtown Brunswick. "In fact, you're glowing."

A wide smile she couldn't suppress emerged on Brooklyn's face as thoughts of the last month she'd spent playing house with Chase—as Zaria called it—soared through her mind. She loved waking up next to him, making breakfast together, and spending quiet time in the evenings at home or going to the beach since the weather had become a tad cooler and lovebug season had ended. Deciding to live in the moment, she pushed the fact he wouldn't always be there to the back of her brain. Her decision was one she didn't regret, especially when she caught him staring at her with an adoration which made her feel like the only woman in the world. This was exactly what she'd always wanted with Chase. A chance to test the waters and see if he was all she imagined. And he was. Even though her heart winced at the thought of him going back to Memphis, she decided to place it out of her mind and whatever happens, happens.

"I'm happy with my decision even if it is temporary, but you and Zaria are definitely the ones glowing." Brooklyn grimaced and shook her head no at a pink, puffy dress the bride-to-be held up. While salmon pink was Reagan's color of choice for the bridal party, she wanted each bridesmaid as well as the maid and matron of honor to wear a dress that fit their style and body type. Today they were gathering ideas to present to the other ladies in the bridal party before they all met at the store next week. Reagan wanted everyone to love and be comfortable in their own selected dress as long as it was salmon pink.

Placing the dress back on the rack, Reagan selected a straight, strapless one. "I think Zaria maybe …"

"Yep, I think so, too," Brooklyn agreed with a knowing wink. "I'm sure she'll tell us when it's the right time."

"As for you, I'm glad you finally came to your senses … well, halfway, but at least you aren't letting that hunk of chocolate go to waste even if it's temporary, I suppose." Reagan shrugged her shoulders, and handed off a few dresses to the sales girl who approached and scurried away to the dressing room where a couple of more dresses awaited. "All ready for your trip to Destin tomorrow?"

"Yes, and I'm so excited!" Brooklyn chose an empire-styled, flowy dress, and Reagan smiled with approval. If Zaria was indeed expecting, this style would be ideal for her. Brooklyn draped it over her arm with three others, and they headed toward the dressing room.

"I'm sure you are. Chase is going with you."

"That too. But I'm also looking forward to shooting Kameryn's latest glass art collection."

"Right. You don't have to worry about bridezillas, moody flower girls, and hung-over groomsmen itching to sprint to the buffet table and open bar."

"Exactly. Glass art can't gripe, complain, become antsy, or talk back. However, I have to obtain the right angles and lighting in order to capture the true essence of the exhibit. Plus, Kameryn has the final approval."

"Everything will go smoothly. You have an eye for this. Can't wait to see the finished book. This could definitely lead to other creative projects."

"That would be nice, but I still wouldn't mind shooting people as well sometimes, or mentoring and teaching future photographers," Brooklyn stated, opening the dressing room door. Her mind trekked back to the building for sale in downtown Memphis. "All right, let's see how many dresses you make me try on today, madam bridezilla."

"While I'm nothing of the sort, I will say I don't like the cut of this one for you."

"I won't try it on."

"I'll go grab some more."

"Perfect," Brooklyn said with a half-laugh as she shut the door.

*

Later on that evening, Brooklyn placed the last of her clothes in the suitcase and set it by the front door next to her camera equipment. Chase was at the kitchen table grading midterms and snacking on carrot sticks with bleu cheese dressing. He was off for fall break, and she was elated he would be able to accompany her to Destin. Shopping for bridal party dresses with Reagan reminded Brooklyn that while she was happy in the moment with Chase, their relationship wasn't going to end up with her planning a wedding with him. Though she could imagine being his wife and spending a lifetime together. Her heart skipped a beat before thumping hard against her chest. Brooklyn shook her head at the craziness she was putting herself through; however, in the end she'd have to suck up the hurt, lock that chapter forever, and move on with her life.

Get it together, girl. This was your bright idea, remember?

Taking her camera out of its bag, Brooklyn treaded lightly to the kitchen entrance so she wouldn't disturb him and switched off the flash. She snapped a few pictures to remember their quiet times like these where they were doing separate tasks but fully aware of the other person.

"I see you, Brook," he whispered, still staring intently at an exam before marking it and grabbing the next one.

"I know."

"You can join me."

"Nope. I know you need to finish before we leave, and I need to make sure I have everything for the trip. The car service will be here promptly at six in the morning to take us to the private airport. Kameryn is a stickler for punctuality, so I need to make sure everything is in place."

A devilish grin crossed his face. "You packed bikinis?" He looked up, tossed the pen on the table, and leaned back in his chair.

"Yes, but I was referring to work related items."

"Can't wait to see you in your true element."

She tilted her head to the side. "You've seen me at plenty of weddings and events. Couldn't take your eyes off of me," she said, remembering the times she'd peek through her camera and catch him staring at her with a delicious smile. She would snap a quick picture before turning away.

"Mmm ... yes, but this will be more of a creative type of project. Your *true* calling."

Brooklyn simply nodded her head because he was right. She was never excited over a wedding unless she knew the bride and groom. Otherwise, it was simply a job she dreaded waking up for.

A light tap at the patio door sent their attention to it as it opened, and Addison stuck her head inside with one hand covering her eyes, wearing a mischievous smirk.

"Is it safe to come in? Are ya'll naked?"

"No, Journey," Chase replied, with a half-laugh. "It's safe to come in."

"Okay, cool," Addison said, entering the kitchen and heading straight to the freezer. "I'm not used to having to peep in. Brooklyn rarely has male company. I wanted to grab the rest of the shrimp from the freezer for dinner before I head to the midnight bowling event I set up for the teachers' association. They needed to release stress on a Friday night."

"Girl, I don't know how you do it," Brooklyn said, sitting next to Chase. "But you're young."

"I enjoy what I do ... for now."

"That's right," Chase teased. "You'll find something else eventually, and I guess it won't be law school."

"You got that right," Addison answered matter-of-factly, leaning against the counter next to the refrigerator. "Brook, did you and Reagan select bridal party dresses today?"

"We perused the samples. I tried on about twenty since I won't be with you guys next week. Today she wanted to view the samples of Elle Lauren's latest collection in person. Elle is personally designing Reagan's wedding dress."

"Cool. Glad she decided to marry on St. Simons after all. An intimate island wedding is perfect."

"Reagan and Blake love the beach. They are truly beach bums. I want my wedding at my family's church where my parents were married."

"For real?" Addison switched her eyes back and forth at her brother and Brooklyn. "Well, alrighty then. Send me an invite you two lovebugs." She winked and skipped out the backdoor with her frozen bag of shrimp.

Brooklyn turned her head to hide the flushness washing over her face like a tidal wave. The image of gliding down the aisle in her mother's dress to marry Chase trampled through her mind. She immediately stood to make her way to anywhere away from him, but he reached out his hand to hers, settling her on his lap.

"Not so fast. Church wedding? My mother will love it… and you. Just tell me what time to be there and where you want to go on our honeymoon. Paris is nice. Or maybe Madrid."

Chase said it so seriously, for a moment she believed him. "Ha ha. I wasn't referring to us. I meant in general. Wait. You think your mother would like me?" *It doesn't matter, and this conversation is pointless,* she thought.

"I said *love* not like. She'd adore you. You're independent and goal-oriented like her. She would appreciate the fact you're chasing your dream of creative photography and not settling for something you don't have the heart for. She's actually on Addi's side about not following in the family's footsteps. I admire that about you as well. I know when I move back to Memphis this is over according to you, but I'd still like to know about your career decisions and when you decide to finally leave Precious Moments."

Brooklyn hadn't thought about life after him and whether or not they would remain in contact. She had assumed they wouldn't for it would make it harder. "Sure,

I can do that," she replied, sliding off his lap, glad the wedding talk nonsense was over.

"Great," he said, opening a folder and pulling out a booklet. "I have a few more midterms to grade."

"I'll let you get back to it. Going to my office to double check my list. I can't have any mistakes this time."

"Hmm … I need to finish packing," he said as if he just remembered. "It won't take long. Just tossing some shorts and casual shirts in my suitcase. Oh, and my golf clubs."

Swiping a bottled water from the refrigerator, she headed toward the stairs of her home office. "Don't forget the swim trunks," she called out. "Oh, wait. You can leave them here. The beach house we rented has an indoor pool. We can go skinny dipping."

"Now I know why I love you, babe. You have the best ideas."

Brooklyn froze at the bottom of the staircase and tightened her grip on the banister when he said the "L" word. It was a phrase she'd heard Chase use before with Addison and on the phone with a friend. However, he had never said it to her, and while he probably didn't mean anything by it, for some reason it was on the tip of her tongue to say it back. She heard papers rustling and carrot crunching, so clearly he was back to grading midterms and not waiting for a "I love you, too" response. Shaking her head at the paranoia she was placing herself in, she jetted to her office.

Later that night, Brooklyn laid nestled in Chase's warm, secure embrace as he rested peacefully against her back in a sound sleep. However, she was wide awake, still brewing over the "L" word and how it was still on the tip of her tongue to tell him. Falling in love with Chase had been her fear all along, and one of the reasons she tried to stop their courtship cold turkey. However, deep down she was drawn to him since the moment they'd met. Nevertheless, this predicament was her own fault. She should've continued admiring him from afar, but she had to have him and now was restraining herself from telling him the three little words which would roll effortlessly through her lips.

Chapter Fourteen

"It's a wrap!" Brooklyn yelled out as she snapped the last picture of the Creatures of the Sea exhibit at the Fine Arts Gallery in Destin, Florida. She shook hands with the two lighting techs she hired to assist with the shoot. "You guys were amazing with helping me capture the right spirit of the exhibit. And we finished in the nick of time. The doors open in an hour. Let's take this stuff out of here."

Once all the equipment was packed and secured in the van, she headed back inside to the lobby, where she spotted Kameryn reviewing last minute details with the museum staff. The private showing and cocktail party was that evening for local VIPs and the press. The doors officially opened tomorrow for the general public. Brooklyn was staying to take pictures of the event for an hour before heading home to change and have dinner with Chase. He'd sent a text earlier stating he missed her and couldn't wait for her to witness the evening he'd planned for them. She hadn't seen him since leaving for the museum at seven in the morning, and he was off to the golf course to play a few rounds with his frat brother who lived not far on Hamilton Island.

"We're all done," Brooklyn informed Kameryn once the staff scattered to their positions.

"I can't wait to see the photos." Kameryn clapped her hands rapidly. "This experience has been wonderful, and I'm even enjoying all the perks." She glanced down at her flowy, white maxi dress. "I may have to keep this one." She winked as the ladies began to stroll along an exhibit of jellyfish following a school of fish. "A local boutique is loaning it out along with the shoes and turquoise jewelry. I have to mention the store on my social media pages."

"It all looks awesome on you," Brooklyn complimented, while remembering her last encounter with jellyfish and Chase's compassion in making sure she was fine followed by the first time they made love. "Definitely your style."

"Thank you. I'm so glad you were able to be here for the private showing. I have another one right before the new year in Memphis. I hope you can attend."

"Yes, your assistant sent me the information."

"Perfect. It was a last minute request from the botanical gardens for their Christmas Winter Wonderland. Luckily, it's only five pieces. It wasn't on my already overbooked schedule to create, but it will be cool to add to the book."

"No problem. I was going to be home around that time anyway. Rasheed is having his annual New Year's Eve bash."

"Mmm … that's wonderful. I haven't been with my family in years for Christmas, much to my parents' chagrin. They moved to Hamilton Island a few years ago after they retired. My mom is a Hamilton, and we used to spend most summer vacations and Christmas there with my maternal grandparents, so it's like my second home away from Savannah. Christmas is such a big deal on the island with festivals, decorating contests, and tree lightings. One day I'll go, I suppose, but it's a busy time of year for me. However, my parents will be here tonight, and I'm spending the day there tomorrow. Do you go home for Christmas?"

"It's been a few years. Sometimes we have weddings on Christmas Eve, or Rasheed and his family go on vacation until the New Year's Eve bash, so I may spend it with Reagan or Zaria on the island or sometimes alone." She hated to admit the holidays to her weren't as special since her parents died. Rasheed had felt the same way as well until he married and started a family of his own.

"Well, you won't be alone this year thanks to the hunk of chocolate you brought along with you. Girl, if a man ever looked at me the way he looks at you maybe I'd give marriage a try again. I loved the way he held you close to him when we encountered a little turbulence on the flight. So sweet and attentive."

"I'm sure you'll marry again if that's what you desire," Brooklyn encouraged, ignoring her friend's statement about her and Chase. She hadn't mentioned to him she would be in Memphis for the holiday season. He was leaving St. Simons beforehand, thus ending their tryst.

"Girl, please. I'm a self-proclaimed workaholic. A husband would just be in my way. My ex divorced me because he said I forgot I was married. Not true, but I don't think we realized how my career—which started as a hobby—would take off overnight, and I found myself working non-stop. But it's fine."

Brooklyn noted a tinge of sorrow in Kameryn's tone as if she was convincing herself she was happy. "I didn't realize you were married before."

"Yep. Straight out of college, but we were high school sweethearts. Lasted three years. We had our wedding at my grandparents' home on Hamilton Island … but that was a lifetime ago." A wistful sigh emerged as she cast her eyes downward for a moment before placing her attention on Brooklyn. "Anyway, what are your plans for the rest of your time here?"

"Not sure. Chase said he's made some plans for us."

"Ah ... how wonderful. You found yourself a keeper. And it's perfect he lives in Memphis."

"Yep. Just perfect," Brooklyn agreed, not wanting to share it didn't matter that he lived in Memphis. She didn't and wasn't going to ever again. "Looks like your guests are beginning to arrive," Brooklyn said as Kameryn's assistant was bringing over a local news crew and patrons began to enter the museum.

"Let the games began," Kameryn stated, readjusting her braids around her shoulders. "Now, don't stay too long. Snap a few pictures of the patrons admiring the exhibit for an hour or so and then skedaddle home to your future husband," Kameryn demanded with a wink before scurrying in the direction of a news anchor who was ready for an interview.

Brooklyn laughed off her friend's last comment, and for the next hour snapped pictures of the event; however, on her way back to the beach rental, her mind couldn't shake the thought of being married to Chase. It wasn't the first time her brain had driven her there, and while she did want to be married one day, it wasn't the end all be all for her. She'd had a couple of long-term relationships, but she wasn't ever upset or even concerned with the fact they didn't end in marriage. Then again, it was never something she'd imagined with any of them ... or at least not in a serious manner, but with Chase she could and it scared her.

Entering the gate of the beach rental, Brooklyn parked the car in the driveway and exhaled in order to rid her head of the nonsense it was filled with. As she slid out of the car, the front door of the house opened and Chase stepped out holding two glasses of what looked like margaritas.

"Welcome home, babe," he said as they met halfway and he handed her the cocktail. "How was your day?"

"It's even better now," she greeted, sipping the cool drink. "This is good. It's been a long but productive day."

"Tired?"

She linked her arm around his strong, taut muscular one as they strolled toward the house. "A little bit but I'm wired so I have some energy left."

"Hungry?"

"Famished. I wolfed down a salad for lunch hours ago."

"I cooked dinner. I figured you'd be too tired to go out."

"Thank you," she said, entering the front door, and the delicious smells of seafood filled her nose. "Did you do a crab boil?"

"Yes, with crab legs, lobster tails, shrimp, sausage, corn on the cob, and new potatoes, along with garlic bread and a salad. Addi, who I called for instructions, said I had to have a green vegetable on the side."

"That sounds wonderful. I'll take a quick shower first."

"Dang, I would love to join you, but I know you need a little me time. I'll meet you out on the deck."

"Okay. And we can always take a shower later on even though I want you to teach me how to play pool first."

He set their glasses on the foyer table and drew her by the waist to him. Dipping his head, he kissed her tenderly on the lips. "I was happily surprised to see the pool table in the game room. Love a woman who knows her man."

There goes that L word again being casually thrown around. Not to mention the fact that he called himself my man. She decided not to dwell on it. "That was one of the reasons why I reserved this place. I saw the pool table in the listing and immediately thought of you. I know how much you like to play."

"I do, and I look forward to teaching you after we devour the crab boil."

"I totally agree."

*****

It was an hour into the pool lesson and so far Brooklyn had managed to poke Chase in the stomach with the pool

139

stick, break a nail, and smear chalk on her face as well as his when he kissed her for actually shooting a ball into the pocket.

"Okay, let's try this again," she said, leaning over the table and positioning the pool stick on the guide ball.

"So, what's the goal?" he asked, kissing the back of her neck and repositioning her hold on the pool stick. "There. That's better. Your arms were bent."

A flutter tingled her insides and she cleared her throat. She peered at him over her shoulder. "Mmm ... see this is why I can't concentrate. You keep finding ways to distract me."

"Sorry, but you're bent over in a short, strapless dress that I'm trying hard not to snatch down. You're the one distracting me, and I don't mind at all. It's a better view than of the ocean from the bedroom."

"Okay ...red ball in right corner pocket."

"You got this," he said, playfully slapping her bottom and stepping back to give her room.

"I see you're standing away from me now."

"Yeah, well I don't want to get jabbed again," he teased, rubbing his left side.

Sliding the pool stick back, she attempted her goal but somehow managed to shoot the white ball up in the air as they both ducked for cover behind the pool table.

"Shoot," she screamed, placing her hands over her head.

Chase peered over the top of the pool table. "Maybe not so hard next time."

"I don't think this pool thing is for me," she said, laughing as they stood up from their stooped down positions on the floor. "Perhaps I should stick to less complex games like Sorry or Checkers."

"Nah, babe," he said, rubbing her back before going to retrieve the ball that landed on the other side of the game room by the ping pong table. "You kind of have the hang of it. I mean, you did manage to shoot one of the balls in the pocket."

"Yeah but it was yours," Brooklyn reminded, placing the stick on the table and leaning against it with a tiny pout and huff.

Setting the ball back on the table, he pulled her in his arms and kissed her forehead. "True, but it's been fun teaching you and gazing at your fine ass bent over," he said, popping her butt. "Especially when your little sundress rose up to display matching hot pink boyshorts." He raised the hem of the dress until it settled on her upper thighs. "I believe right here," he said, clutching her hips in his hands. "Yeah, this is perfect."

"It wasn't that far up," she teased, wrapping her arms around his neck. "But you know we can do more besides play pool on the pool table," she suggested with a wicked grin, and then kissed him softly on the lips.

"Mmm … oh really?" Delving his tongue deeper into her mouth, he captured hers in a slow, erotic tango which elicited moans from both of them.

"Mmm-hmm … see, something like this I'm more apt not to mess up."

"I couldn't agree more," he whispered above her lips before taking possession of them once more, but this time more exaggerated and untamed than ever before.

Brooklyn's body turned into complete putty as the desire pulsating through him to her amplified with each possessive kiss. It signified she belonged solely to him, and the notion of that jolted a strong force of passion to surge to her core. The closer it progressed to the end of the year, the more her heart ached as well as yearned for him at the same time. She hated the roller coaster of emotions her suggestion of just having fun with him while she could wreaked havoc on her to the point of knowing she was truly breaking her own heart. As he gathered her in his arms, and she wrapped her legs around his waist, the sense of belonging and oneness crept upon her. Never had she felt so relaxed and so at home with a man before. When he stopped kissing her for a millisecond to pull down her dress and panties as he'd wanted to do since the pool lesson began, she almost shouted out in protest to place his lips back on hers.

"See, the pool table has come in handy after all," Chase said, lifting her up and setting her on the edge. "Don't worry. I'm not going to let you fall."

Too late. I've fallen all right. Right in love with you, she thought.

"I know." Brooklyn reached into the front pocket of his shorts for the gold packet she'd spotted earlier. "You just keep these around?" she teased, handing it to him.

"I figured we'd need to be prepared no matter where we are," he replied, taking off his shorts and placing the object from the packet on.

"That is so true." With a wink, she turned around and bent over the table.

"Oh ... nice," he murmured, popping her bottom and squeezing his hands on her hips. "One of my favorite views."

Chase kissed the back of her neck as he entered her at the same time. A rush of passion soared through her body, heightening with every single long stroke from him.

"Ch-Chase ... shit ... th-that feels g-good," she managed to stammer out as she gripped the pool table tight while the erotic music they created filled the room.

Brooklyn was glad Chase offered to rent the house as opposed to staying in the condos with the rest of the crew. Her screams of ecstasy grew louder with every single thrust from him over and over, pushing her farther onto the table until her arms were sprawled out on the green felt in front of her. She laid flat with him following on top, not missing a single beat. She pushed the black ball out of the way, and it landed in one of the pockets.

Chase chuckled, kissing the side of her neck. "I guess this is a better way for you to play pool. You just won the game."

"Maybe we should've started like this," she giggled, but it turned into a low moan as he slowed down the pace to a sensual, unhurried rhythm.

Reaching his lips around to hers, he captured them in an untamed kiss that exuded an intense shudder to rage though her. He held her tight against him as their tempo picked back up, crashing into her over and over. Never had a man sent her this far over the edge into an uncanny abyss. Brooklyn couldn't think of a time where she'd felt so aware and in tune with her sexual side, but Chase brought out every sensor on her body to only respond to him.

He continue ravishing her into an oblivious state, and she had no choice but to let go of his mouth in order to release a passionate sound so foreign to her for a second Brooklyn didn't recognize it was her own voice calling out his name as they both climaxed together. Chase buried his head on her shoulder as the shocks from his body simmered down, and their breathing cascaded back to normal.

"Chase?"

"Yeah, babe?" he asked, lifting off of her and positioning them until they lay facing each other.

"You wanna play again?" she whispered.

He frowned. "Uh … you're referring to actually playing pool?"

"Sure, as long as we end up right back here," she replied, kissing him lightly.

"Well, let's rack 'em up!"

Chapter Fifteen

"With the holiday season just around the corner, I wanted to go over the updates for the upcoming events and take a look at everyone's schedule for the new year as well," Reagan explained at the Precious Moments' weekly brunch meeting on her enclosed sunroom since it was a cool, rainy day outside in early December.

Brooklyn heard her best friend, but the words didn't register as she twirled her spoon around in the cheesy polenta topped with Cajun shrimp. Chase was leaving in a week, the day after final exams, to head back to Memphis. She would be there two weeks later for New Year's Eve, but decided to omit that part to him. He hadn't mentioned anything about seeing her again once he left St. Simons because she'd been adamant about not discussing it. Even though that's what she wanted initially, it now pained her heart in ways she couldn't express to him. Their time together was winding down, and he'd been somewhat distant the last couple of days. He seemed rather anxious to head home and begin working with the family law firm. He'd been on conference calls the past week with either his mother or Zoe pertaining to current cases. Obviously he was ecstatic about his partnership in his family's firm and Brooklyn was happy for him. A part of her hated she wouldn't be by his side as he embarked on a new career adventure, but it was a decision she'd have to overcome.

However, she was happy with her own career endeavors and couldn't wait to witness what the new year had in store. The distraction of having Chase in her life had been welcomed, but now it was time to drift back into reality, and she'd begun making plans of her own.

"Brook, are you ready to share your wonderful news with the crew?" Reagan asked in an upbeat tone, glancing around the table at everyone—which included the interns and Kelli, Brooklyn's photographer's assistant.

Brooklyn turned and smiled at Reagan who had already received her official notice of leaving Precious Moments a week prior. Zaria and Reagan bought out Brooklyn's share of the company. The option was extended to Addison as well, but she declined citing she didn't know where the wind would blow her next summer after her contract was up, and she wasn't sure yet about renewing it.

"Yes, of course," Brooklyn began, pausing as she promised herself to remain composed and not become teary-eyed. "As some of you are already aware, I've been contemplating going in a slightly different direction with my career, and in the new year, I will no longer be part owner of Precious Moments Events." She paused again to put her thoughts together while a few of the interns groaned in sadness. "However, I have already agreed to be the photographer of some upcoming weddings through March, so I'm not leaving you guys just yet. Afterward, Kelli will officially take over as the main photographer. I will also assist the new accountant with the budget and whatnot for the first part of the year."

"Well, you already know how happy I am for you," Zaria said, taking a sip of her sparkling water. "I love how you're doing your own thing."

"Me too," Addison chimed in with claps as well as the rest of the staff. "You know I'm all for change."

"Are you going to stay on St. Simons?" Kelli asked.

"Yes, for the time being. Eventually, I want to have a central location where I can open my studio and a gallery of sorts. A classroom, perhaps. They're just ideas, but I'm ready to explore and set things in motion. And it could very well be in the St. Simons/Brunswick area. Not sure. Going to do some more research. By selling my share of the company to Zaria and Reagan, I have a nice little nest egg to buy my studio eventually. In the meantime, I have some projects with Kam that will require travel and a few other things on the horizon. I'm excited to see what the future holds."

"We're all so proud of you." Reagan raised her mimosa in the air as the rest of the ladies followed suit with their champagne glasses and all toasted to Brooklyn.

"Thank you, everyone," Brooklyn said, holding back the tears in the corners of her eyes as her voice became hoarse. She hadn't realized it would be hard to say good-bye, but she'd enjoyed working alongside her best friends. "These last few years with Precious Moments have been a wonderful experience, and I'm still here whenever needed."

All the ladies clapped and took turns giving Brooklyn hugs and offering words of support and well wishes.

"Any other news before we adjourn?" Reagan asked, moments later after everyone settled back in their seats.

Zaria raised her hand. "I have some news to share before we close the meeting."

"We're all ears," Brooklyn said, glancing at Reagan who couldn't contain the wide smile on her face. Brooklyn tried to keep her composure as she struggled to stay in her chair and not run screaming with joy along with Reagan to hug Zaria.

"I received a phone call this morning from the African-American United Golf League. They want to host their annual golf charity tournament here on St. Simons and are requesting Precious Moments to assist with the arrangements," Zaria explained, glancing down at her notes and turning to Addison. "Addi, I think that's something you'd be perfect to oversee. They want a week full of fun events leading up to the charity tournament, which would be that weekend with perhaps an auction or a ball type of event at the end. It's not until this upcoming summer. I'll forward you the information I received from the organization."

"That sounds right up my alley," Addison said, through a clenched smile followed by a heavy sigh. "I'll add it to my schedule."

Brooklyn sensed that Addison's thoughts trekked to her ex who was a pro golfer and probably prayed he wouldn't be in attendance. She was relieved when he didn't show for his cousin's wedding on Hamilton Island. She glanced back at Reagan whose excited face turned into a questionable one. They'd hoped Zaria had a different kind of announcement.

After the interns and Kelli left, the ladies retreated to the outside deck of Reagan's home now that the rain had finally cleared. It was still cool but the noon sun shone brightly on the deck, offering a little heat. They dragged the outdoor chaise lounges from the sunroom while Reagan brought out a pitcher of mimosas and sparkling water along with four champagne glasses all on a tray and set it on the table.

"Drink up, ladies, because the rest of the month is busy busy with holiday parties, two weddings, and that sweet sixteen birthday party I'm not looking forward to," Reagan said, plopping down in a chaise lounge and tucking her feet under her. "And that's all before Christmas. Can't wait for my ski trip to Aspen with Blake. Until then, we hustle."

"Girl, I know but what a way to end a fabulous year," Zaria said, pouring mimosa into a glass and taking a gulp as all eyes stared at her in bewilderment. Topping off her glass, she sat on the chaise next to Reagan and swished her frowned lips to the side. "What's wrong with ya'll?" she asked.

"Oh ... um ... nothing," Brooklyn started. "We just haven't seen you drink alcohol in about four months."

"Yeah, you've turned down margaritas lately," Reagan said. "We thought ... well—"

"We thought you were pregnant and *that* was your big announcement today," Addison said, pouring her a glass of mimosa. "So what's the tea, Z?"

Bursting into laughter, Zaria shook her head in the negative, lifted her sweater, and patted her toned stomach. "Wow, you guys are hilarious. No, you aren't going to be aunties or godmothers just yet. I'm not pregnant, nor was I pregnant. I'm not drinking because we're going to start trying to conceive in the new year. I've been preparing my body. I decided to have a mimosa today since we were toasting the end of the year and new beginnings. That's all, ladies. Calm down."

"That's still wonderful news, Zaria," Reagan said. "I know you and Garrett will make awesome parents."

"Thank you. We're excited and nervous, but we're ready. Now I know why everyone's been eyeing me crazy and glancing down at my stomach. Humph ... that empire-styled dress that Reagan suggested for her wedding," Zaria said, giving Reagan a playful nudge.

"Yeah, I was concerned when you selected the straight one," Reagan replied with a teasing wink.

"We're just ready for someone to have a little nugget," Addison interjected, scooting Zaria over in the chaise lounge with her hips. She rubbed Zaria's stomach. "Now, can you imagine a little Z prancing around here like her sassy momma telling everyone what to do and what she's not going to do?"

"Oh, no," Brooklyn said with a grimace followed by a giggle. "I've known Z since elementary school, and trust me, she has always had a mouth. The mouth of the south is what Rasheed used to call her. I don't know if we can handle two Zarias."

"Whatever," Zaria snapped playfully, putting her hand in the halting position in the air. "Baby Z or G will be just fine ... but yeah, hopefully she's not as bad as me."

"I agree," Brooklyn said, pulling her camera out of her tote bag to snap pictures of her friends. The thought of not being with them tugged at her heart, and she wanted to commemorate all their fun and precious moments together for as long as possible.

After she snapped a few pictures and showed them to the ladies, Addison snatched the camera out of Brooklyn's hands.

"I know. I know." Taking a step back, Addison cradled the camera close to her chest. "No one is allowed to touch your precious camera, but while perusing through the pictures, I realized you weren't in them except for a few selfies. I love being a part of the group, but the three of you are childhood best friends ... no, you're practically sisters, and it's only befitting that there's pictures with just the three of you who started this business years ago and made the success that it is. So, skedaddle over there on the lounge chair and pose with your besties, Brooklyn."

"Will do, Addi, and thank you." Brooklyn's forehead scrunched as Addi eyed the functions on the camera. "Just press the red button at the top," she instructed.

"Got it," Addi said. "Okay, ladies. Say sistas for life!"

*****

Brooklyn yawned as she prepared the ham and herb omelet to serve along with her mother's Sunday biscuits. It wasn't Sunday, but Chase was leaving soon to drive the eleven hours to Memphis and she wanted to make sure he had a hearty breakfast. Addison was tagging along to attend a friend's birthday party and would fly back two days later in time for a work event. Brooklyn was cooking breakfast for the three of them, but she had no appetite. Yawning again, she glanced at the clock on the microwave that read six-thirty in the morning. She didn't sleep well last night, but instead dozed off and on as he held her snug against his chest as if he wasn't ever letting her go. In between his soft snoring, he'd wake up, kiss her on the forehead or cheek, and pull her even tighter against him.

The alarm of the front door chimed as Chase went in and out to pack his luggage into the trunk of his car. The tugging in her heart pained every beat. Hearing the click of the lock caused a slight dizziness to cascade over her as it signaled he was done. Small things such as that were weighing heavy on her as the time drew near for him to leave her life.

Blinking her eyelashes rapidly to ward off the tears that wanted to fall, Brooklyn flipped the omelet onto a platter with the other two and turned off the stove. Opening the lid to the cheese grits, she stirred them to make sure they were creamy and smooth just the way he liked them. The coffee maker beeped, and she poured a cup while yawning again. She took a sip just as comforting arms wrapped around her waist and a tender kiss on the neck commissioned a sigh to exhale from them both. The fresh shower scent mingled with Chase's cologne aroused her senses. She held in another sigh that wanted to escape as it occurred to her this would be the last time his scent filled her atmosphere. Scooting out of his cocoon, Brooklyn grabbed the platters of food and set them on the kitchen table that was set just as it was the morning they'd first ate breakfast together months before. He swiped the pot of grits and placed it on top of the trivet on the table.

"Here you go, beautiful," Chase offered, holding out her chair.

She turned toward the refrigerator to grab the butter and jam. "I'm not hungry at the moment but eat up. Addi will be here in a little bit." Brooklyn hoped soon so the awkwardness soaring through her veins could end. She didn't think it would be so hard to say good-bye to him for she'd tried to write it off as just a fall fling, but her heart was screaming otherwise.

"I stopped by Addi's while I was outside. She just woke up and will be over in thirty minutes or so. She's not even packed," he said, ending with a sarcastic laugh.

Leaning against the counter, Brooklyn sipped her coffee while trying to hold in her tears. "Well, you know Addi hitches her house up to her truck and hits the road with all her belongings in tow."

"Yeah, you're right."

"Car all packed?" she asked, trying to prolong the inevitable conversation that was written all over his face. Last night, she sensed he wanted to talk about their relationship continuing past today after they made love, but she yawned a few times, citing she was tired, and pretended to fall asleep.

"Yep," he answered, spreading butter over his biscuit. "Hmm ... this reminds me of our first date. You cooked breakfast for us."

She laughed lightly and joined him at the table. "I was already making breakfast for me and it wasn't a date," she reminded. She wasn't hungry but found herself making a small plate just to keep her nerves occupied.

"But it was perfect timing. I enjoyed that day ... I've enjoyed all of our days and nights together since then."

"Me too," she answered, scared of where this conversation could head.

"But you still ..." He stopped with the bread in his hand midway in the air.

"Yes. I think it's best."

"You know where I am if you change your mind," Chase said, popping the piece of biscuit in his mouth and taking a sip of his orange juice.

Nodding, she took a bite of her cheese grits so she wouldn't have to verbally answer.

"You have to visit Memphis sometime," he said as if he knew the thought in her head. "Your family is there."

"Yes, my brother and his family are there."

"Okay. I won't press you anymore. I know we agreed … I just hadn't totally given up. When you find that special someone to spend the rest of your life with, you don't give up …especially when you know she feels the exact same way. However, you've made your feelings clear because of your own personal reasons."

"Chase … I …" Brooklyn stumbled and stopped as her heart began to race.

A light rap at the backdoor was followed by it opening, and Addison sticking her head in.

"Is it safe to enter?" she asked, covering her eyes with her hand but leaving a slot open to peek through. "Just wanted to make sure ya'll weren't on the kitchen table getting in one last tryst or something. Wait, you haven't actually done it there have you? I do eat on it, you know."

Laughing, Brooklyn shook her head. "Girl, get in here," she said, motioning with her hand, grateful Addison appeared when she did. "Breakfast is still hot, and I packed lunch for you two as well. Chicken salad croissants, fruit salad, and other goodies to tide you over for twelve hours so you don't have to eat fast food."

Strolling in with a duffle bag on her back, Addison placed it on the floor next to the backdoor before joining them at the table. She glanced at Chase while pouring coffee into a mug and gave him a thoughtful pout.

"I can eat at home and come back when you're ready to leave if you guys need some more alone time," Addison suggested, eyeing Chase and Brooklyn back in forth. "Just call," she said, sliding an omelet on her plate.

"No," Chase said in an abrupt tone. "We'll leave after breakfast. I gassed up the car last night and all of my suitcases are in the trunk. I saved a spot for yours."

"I'll drive first," Addison offered, studying his face which held a clenched jaw. "I purposely went to sleep early last night."

"Nah, just relax for awhile," he answered, digging into his omelet. "I'll drive."

Brooklyn noticed the solemn expression he was trying to hide, but she knew he was probably glad Addison had arrived as well as the conversation would veer downhill if they continued to talk.

Brooklyn didn't want to end their relationship on a bad note. Honestly, she thought this would be easy considering they agreed to have fun while he was here. But what did she do? She fell harder than expected, causing her mind and heart to be in a topsy turvy state, and now Chase barely wanted to look at her.

They ate and chatted for the next thirty minutes with Addison doing most of the talking about her next adventure at the end of the year which included climbing down an active waterfall.

"Everything was delish, Brook," Addison complimented, scooting her chair back and standing. Swiping hers and Chase's empty dishes from the table, she headed to the sink.

"Thank you. Just set them on the counter. I'm going to toss everything in the dishwasher when you guys leave." *And then cry like a baby.*

"We should hit the road in about ten minutes, Addi," Chase said with a slight rumble in his throat. "I'll go ahead and place your belongings in the car."

"Okay." Addison hesitated, glancing at Brooklyn who was clearing the rest of the dishes from the table. "I forgot my ereader, and since you're driving first I can finish reading the latest Phyllis Bourne novel," she announced, turning on her heel and making long strides to the door. "I'll be back in a bit."

Once Addison left, Brooklyn began loading the dishwasher to hide the sadness that swept through every cell in her body. It was sinking in that Chase would be out of her life for good within the next few moments. While she knew it was her decision, it hurt as if it wasn't. She was breaking her own heart, but she figured it would be easier to do it now as opposed to starting a relationship that would end with them breaking up because they'd never live in the same city.

Warm hands encircled her waist and turned her around. Intense eyes bore into hers with a string of emotions all rolled into one. Anger, adoration, and puzzlement were etched on his face. He placed his forehead on hers and breathed out a long-winded groan. She tried to keep calm. No matter what she wasn't going to let him see her cry. That wasn't the last image of her she wanted him to have. Instead, she kissed him lightly on the lips and smiled through the pain crushing her chest like a two-ton weight.

"I'm going to miss you, Chase. My time with you was precious and everything I knew it would be since the moment we met."

He inhaled and glanced away from her for a second. She sensed he wanted to ask her one more time to reconsider. Instead, Chase shook his head as if he knew her answer would be in the negative.

"The time we shared will forever be engraved on my heart, Brooklyn," he said tenderly against her lips. "I will hate every moment when we're apart. You will always be very special to me, no matter what happens in the future. I hope everything you want out of life happens."

"Thank you, Chase, and I wish the same for you. I know you'll succeed in this new journey, as well."

"Thank you."

"I guess ... we should ... uh ... say good-bye now." Her voice cracked over the words as true reality sunk in.

Placing his hands on either side of her face, he stared into her eyes as his welled with tears. "I'm not saying good-bye. Instead, I'll say see you later ... hopefully sooner than later."

Before she could answer, he landed a deep, possessive kiss on her lips, causing her entire body to tremble against his. Her heart broke into a million pieces at that very instant.

"I guess it's that time," Brooklyn said, pulling away from his embrace. However, he held her firm to him.

"Back to reality," he whispered with a shudder. "I'm going to miss this. Miss us, baby."

Brooklyn pulled away again as the tears wanted to escape misty eyes and the voice in her head that screamed so loud she was sure even he could hear it saying, *"Don't let him get away."* Chase released her from the safety of his arms, causing her lungs to stop compressing, but she couldn't worry about it now. It was all over just like that.

She heard Addi's voice in the distance talking on the phone in an upbeat manner. Walking to the backdoor, Brooklyn opened it to let in Addi, who zoned in on her friend's face and gave her a warm, comforting hug.

"Okay, girlie," Addison started in a chipper voice, "I'll miss your home-cooked meals. I'm staying with Zoe, and she doesn't cook … okay, she does but not that great," she stated, laughing. "But she's great at ordering food, though,"

Brooklyn laughed back which she knew that's what Addison wanted her to do to lighten the mood. "It's only three days."

"I know, but obviously you've never had Zoe's cooking …" Addison said, squeezing Brooklyn again before letting go. She turned toward Chase who was lifting the pull handle of the ice chest with their lunch. "You ready to head back to Memphis?" she asked. "You have a law firm to run, big brother."

"Ready as I'll ever be," Chase answered, heading to the front door with the ladies on his heels.

"All right, you two," Brooklyn said, opening the front door, letting the travelers pass through. "Have a safe trip." She stayed on the porch instead of following them out to the car. She wanted to hug him one last time, but she knew she'd turn on the waterworks at the highest level, and she didn't want that to be his last memory. Instead, Brooklyn waved good-bye and turned back inside of the house before they left the driveway. Peeking out the window, she watched until she could no longer see the taillights of Chase's BMW and that's when she skedaddled back to her bed, engulfed herself in her sheets that still held his intoxicating scent, and let out a long, hard cry over the biggest mistake she'd ever made in her life.

Chapter Sixteen

"So how do you like your new office with Wentworth, Arrington, and Associates?" Zoe asked, opening the double doors and stepping aside to let Chase enter onto the shiny walnut hardwood. "As you can see, we did some renovations since your last visit considering this used to be Mother's old office." She stood in the middle of the corner office on the fifth floor which overlooked an expansive view of the Mississippi River and the Hernando de Soto bridge that led to West Memphis, Arkansas. "Well?" she asked, sliding her hands in the pockets of her black palazzo dress slacks. "We didn't think you'd want antique white wallpaper with pink tea roses and cream carpet."

"Ha, no. Not at all." Chase chuckled in agreement as his eyes scanned the rich wood paneled walls with matching crown molding that ran in the middle to make an architectural design. Empty bookcases flanked the two walls without floor to ceiling windows that were luckily tinted to block out the glaring morning sun that had just been in his eyes while he drove to work. He had a ton of law books and souvenirs from his recent travels abroad during the first half of his sabbatical to fill the shelves. On the left side of the room was a sitting area with a chocolate-colored leather couch with a matching love seat perfect for his long nights ahead with cases, and he'd need a spot to nap. On the opposite side, was a round conference table with four chairs for meetings or spreading out his work. The focal point, however, was the antique wood, hand-carved desk which once belonged to his great-grandfather, Hunter Wentworth, who'd started the firm decades ago. Chase had always admired the desk of the man he never knew, but had heard and read countless stories of how his great-grandfather started the law firm during a time when African-Americans were still not completely welcomed in the field. It was one of the reasons he wanted to carry on the family legacy and make sure this mother's grandfather was never forgotten.

"Everything is perfect," he said, running his hand along the top of the fine wood and walking around it in awe. He used to sit there as a teenager when his mother wasn't in her office, and pretend it was his. "I'm surprised Mom is giving it to me." The last time he worked there after law school, his desk was a fake wood desk picked out of an office furniture catalog.

"Well she's retired now and figured you would appreciate it. I have granddaddy Wentworth's desk."

"Ah ... I see," Chase said, taking a seat in the leather swivel chair. His eyes rested on an 8x10 family portrait of him, his parents, and siblings that he was sure his mother had placed there for him. The brass frame engraved with 'The Arringtons' in calligraphy was much too fancy for his taste, but he definitely wasn't going to switch it to another one. "Your favorite person in the whole world."

Zoe sat in one of the brown leather chairs in front of the desk and crossed her legs. "He was a great man and such a sweetheart ... well, maybe not in the courtroom but with us, he was the funniest man alive. I miss him and his corny jokes."

"Yeah, me too, sis," he agreed, remembering their grandfather's hearty laugh after he told his jokes whether they were funny or not. "I'm glad you and I are able to carry on the family legacy."

"Yes, and speaking of family legacies, I heard back from the private investigator I hired to look into Uncle Sean's life."

"Really?" Chase asked, taking off his blue suit jacket and draping it over the back of the chair. "What did he say?"

"We have another cousin," Zoe announced with a clap her hands. "Her name is Giselle Arrington. She's thirty, single, and no children. She lives in Laurelville, a small town in Connecticut outside of Hartford, and she's a romance writer but under a pen name."

"Cool. So she's not a lawyer or a doctor, huh?" Chase questioned. "Wait, is her mother an author, too?"

"No, but her mother has recently passed. Apparently, they married before his first tour of duty when they were barely twenty, but it turned tumultuous when he returned. She divorced him when Giselle was a baby, cutting off all contact, and moved to Laurelville. Uncle Sean did a few more tours of duty before moving back to Memphis. I spoke to Dad this morning about it. He said he and Uncle Frances never knew their baby brother had a family, though he was suffering from severe PTSD and was on drugs. The investigator gave me Giselle's contact information. I reached out last night, but she hasn't returned my call yet."

"Have you told anyone else in the family?"

"No. I'm going to wait until I hear back, if I hear back. She never searched for us so maybe she doesn't want to be in contact."

"And we'll have to respect that," Chase said with a wistful shrug of his shoulders. "Perhaps she didn't know or want to search for us. Who knows what her mother told her about her father."

"True, so I won't press the issue if she wants to be left alone." Zoe paused for a moment as a strained frown emerged on her face. "Have you spoken to Brooklyn since you returned?" she asked in a soft, comforting voice.

It had been a week since he returned to Memphis and Brooklyn stayed heavy on his mind. He'd assumed once he returned home, she would be out of his system because he needed to become acclimated once again to his normal life. He figured meetings with Zoe and his mother as she officially turned over the reins of the firm to them and catching up with his friends would keep him occupied. Instead, tasks such as dusting off his pool table only reminded him of their time in Destin, and when they made love when he was supposed to be teaching her how to play pool.

Sleep wasn't easy either as he'd grown accustomed to holding Brooklyn in his arms and listening to her soft snores. Waking up with her sleepy yet beautiful eyes on him or the smell of fresh biscuits baking every Sunday morning had spoiled him to no end.

"No ... and I'm not going to call her." Chase eyed his sister carefully for he was positive Zoe was going to say he should and stop being petty. "She has to decide for herself what she wants. I'm not going to force her or beg her to be with me. Brooklyn knows she owns my heart."

"If it's meant to be, then it's meant to be." Zoe paused again, breathing in deep and tapping her finger on her chin.

Chase tilted his head to the side as he studied Zoe. She always said exactly what was on her mind so he was taken aback by her contemplation mode all of sudden. "Spill it, sis."

"Um ... I heard she may be in Memphis for Rasheed's New Year's Eve bash."

He tried to keep a straight face as the jolt in his heart nearly knocked him over. "Oh ... I see," he said, trying to disguise the disappointment in his tone which didn't work as Zoe's eyes saddened.

"I guess you didn't know."

"No. She mentioned she had to work during the holiday season on St. Simons. It's not like we made plans to see each other if she was in the city, but—"

"Maybe it was a last minute decision," she suggested. "I'm sorry. I shouldn't have told you."

"It's cool … I mean, it's her city, too, and her brother's party. Addi told you?"

"No. Bria mentioned at lunch the other day that Brooklyn would be in town in time for the party."

"I guess I'll see her there, and uh … you'll see someone, too." He had to change the subject to avoid the pain swelling in his chest. He'd hope there was some chance that Brooklyn would want to see him whenever she visited.

Narrowing her eyes at him, Zoe's mouth pursed into a sarcastic smirk. "Who?"

"Aiden Graham," he answered, referring to Langston's older brother who was a sports analyst on the show *Sports Fanatic*.

Smacking her lips, she shook her head. "Here we go again. You're worse than Addi. We went on one date and you all swear it was a match made in heaven. Mother swore she was going to plan a double wedding for me and Addi to two brothers which will never happen because baby sis hates her ex, and I have no interest in his brother. He's a nice guy, but he's not my type." Standing, Zoe pivoted toward the door. "Why do you think he'll be there?" she asked, her tone laced in curiosity.

"Mmm-hmm." Chase smirked at her question. "He's the emcee for the event. I guess you didn't read the invite. And I know you like those pretty boy types like Rick Foxx and Shemar Moore. Al B. Sure."

"Whatever. And those men are old enough to be my daddy. I'm only twenty-seven but Rick Foxx is fine. Stick to your day job and stop playing matchmaker. Anyway, I need to go to the satellite office in Germantown and you have a meeting with Human Resources or you won't get paid."

"All right. Thank you for the information about Brook."

"Knowledge is power, but it doesn't matter if you don't use it." Zoe winked, walking out of the double doors and closing them behind her.

Chase leaned back in his chair as his eyes landed on the bare wall opposite where his desk sat. It needed some spicing up if he was going to have to see it in front of him every day. He figured artwork such as black and white creative photography could add a touch of character, and his mind transported him back to the black and white pictures in the hallway of Brooklyn's home. Too bad he couldn't just call her up and ask if she had any creative photos in her portfolio she could blow up and frame for him. However, he'd promised himself he wasn't going to reach out to her and not in a stubborn way as Zoe assumed. He'd wanted to respect Brooklyn's wishes, but now knowing they were going to be at the same party on New Year's Eve, the perfect plan formed in his head.

*****

"Burrr…" Brooklyn said with a shiver as she stepped out of the back of Rasheed's Maybach. She nodded to his long-time driver and met her brother on the other side of the black luxury sedan as he pulled a container of purple and gold winter-flowering pansies out of the front seat.

"It's a little chilly," he said, winking as they stepped onto the sidewalk that led to their destination. Shifting the container on one arm, he pulled a black remote out of his coat pocket and aimed it in front of him.

"I don't miss this cold weather at all," she stated, pulling the trench coat closer as the cold Memphis wind blew strong against her.

For some reason, tossing a winter coat into the suitcase had escaped her mind when packing for the trip, and she'd borrowed one of Bria's for the outing with Rasheed.

However, for the past few weeks, Brooklyn's life had been one big blur of winter weddings, Christmas parties, and a last minute photo shoot with a newly engaged couple which she'd conducted an hour before boarding her brother's private jet to head to Memphis to meet Kameryn at the Botanical Gardens. On the outside she was bubbly, perhaps over bubbly, and proclaiming to be in good spirits to suppress the pain living in her heart. Being in her hometown reminded Brooklyn of missing her parents, but it also reminded her that the man she loved lived there. She needed to call him and hear his soothing voice in her ear. She needed to tell him she missed him like crazy and wanted to give them a chance.

Wrapping her hand around Rasheed's arm, he offered a comforting smile as he pressed a button on the remote. They entered the black wrought iron gates of the small, private garden memorial they'd created for their parents at the cemetery. The pink camellia bushes had just started to bloom, as they were in her opinion winter roses, and she'd suggested them so flowers would always grace the garden no matter the season.

"Nope. I don't miss this weather at all," Brooklyn repeated, wrapping the scarf that had once belonged to Chase tighter around her neck. Stopping in her tracks, she pushed her gloved hands into the coat pockets as her heartbeat sped up. "Mhmmm," she sighed, saddened to see her parents' names on their tombstones. "But I do miss them. Very much. Sometimes it feels like a bad dream that I can't awake from no matter how hard I try." She stooped down in front of her mother's grave and ran a finger along her name written in a calligraphy print.

"Me too," Rasheed answered, setting the container of pansies between the tombstones and heading to the bench nearby. "It's not that cold, Brooklyn," he teased as she stood back up and began to jog in place.

"Look, I've lived by the beach for the last few years," she reminded, joining him on the bench wishing she had her coffee that was in the car. "Though I am excited about the possibility of snow tonight. Now *that* I do miss. Regardless, I have to get used to this type of cold weather again."

He turned toward her wearing a wide grin that seemed to stretch all the way up to his bald head. "Again? Uh huh. Soooooooo, is Memphis on the list of places to open your photography studio now that you're leaving Precious Moments?"

"I didn't say that," she quipped, not ready to share her possible plans yet. "I just meant in general."

"You know that empty building in downtown we saw the last time you were here is still available."

"It's ideal … um … something like it."

Brooklyn hadn't been able to shake the place out of her head and had pulled up the information and floor plans on the real estate agent's website countless times. The layout and location of the studio was perfect. She'd researched similar places in the cities on her list including the St. Simons/Brunswick area and had visited a few. However, she found fault with all of them. None of them compared to the one in downtown Memphis and she couldn't wait to lay eyes on it again.

"Look, I'm not trying to convince you to move back here if you don't want to, but I know you miss being here. I know you hate the fact that our parents are no longer with us; however, they're in our hearts no matter where you live. Perhaps living away from home makes it a tad easier for you."

"Honestly, I thought it would be but no, it's the same pain. The truth is, I'd needed a change of scenery after I finished my master's degree. I was in limbo doing photography on the side and working at that huge accounting firm where I was just another CPA. I needed something new and exciting to do, so when Reagan asked me to join her and Zaria with Precious Moments, it was the perfect opportunity. I enjoyed being there and helping my girlfriends with their dream, but it wasn't my vision for myself."

"You've talked about opening a studio and mentoring aspiring creative photographers for as long as I can remember. I'm proud of you for pursuing your own dreams, and if you need anything, I got you. You want that studio downtown? Say the word. It's yours."

She smiled at her brother. He'd spoiled her for as long as she could remember. However, this was something she needed to on her own. "Honestly, I do want the studio downtown, but you don't have to buy it for me. I have my own money you know."

"Fine." He slid his cellphone out of his pocket. "Can your big brother at least call and set up an appointment with the real estate agent so you can see it in person while you're in town?"

"Too late." Standing, she pulled him off the bench. "That's where we're going next," she said with a definite smile. "I've already made the appointment."

"Okay, I forgot how take charge you are. Just like Mom."

"I'm not saying I'm putting a contract on it today, but I've been dying to see it again. I think then I can make a final decision."

"And Chase?" Rasheed asked, as they walked out of the garden. Turning, he pressed the remote to close the gates. "Are you dying to see him as well?"

"Yes. I miss him like crazy, and I know he's the one for me." She loved to acknowledge it out loud and couldn't wait to tell Chase in person, but she needed to handle her business first.

"Ah ... so he's the real reason you're contemplating moving back home?" he asked as they followed the path to his car.

"Yes and no. This career change and moving back to Memphis is something I've been wrestling with before he and I had a relationship ... well, whatever it was. However,

I miss you and I hate missing important events in you and your family's lives. When I saw the empty studio the last time I was home, something clicked. I can't stop thinking about it, and all the possibilities that will come with it. So, no Chase isn't the *only* reason."

"He'll be at the party tonight," Rasheed said as they reached his Maybach.

"Oh, that's perfect. I was going to call him, but I'll surprise him."

"I'm sure Chase will be over the moon to see you." Rasheed opened the back door for Brooklyn. "Now let's jet to this meeting so I can do my damnedest to convince you to buy this place, and if its not up to par, we'll find you another one. Or I'll have one built for you. My baby sister is moving home!" Rasheed exclaimed, giving her a bear hug.

"Ha ha! We'll see," Brooklyn said, squeezing him back before sliding onto the black leather wearing a smile. For in her heart she finally knew exactly what she wanted to do and was at peace with her decision.

Chapter Seventeen

Brooklyn's heart raced as the Maybach came to a halt in front of the VIP drop off at Lillian's Dinner and Blue's Club that evening for the annual New Year's Eve bash. There were a few more cars in front of her, and she appreciated the wait. Breathing in deeply, she sipped the last of her champagne and placed the empty glass in the cup holder between the two oversized, leather executive seats. She was alone with her thoughts as Rasheed and Bria had left an hour before because they were co-hosting the event.

Brooklyn was relieved to have time to reflect before tonight's festivities. Since arriving in Memphis, she'd been running non-stop from working with Kameryn, visiting her parents' final resting place, touring the studio, and hurrying back to Rasheed's mansion to prepare for the party including trying on over a dozen dresses. Dressing in formal attire had never been her forte. Usually at events, she was the photographer and would remain low key in a pair of dress slacks and a blouse. She'd offered to be the main photographer but Rasheed refused. In a way she was relieved, but it was the habit of volunteering she had to break. Tonight was about starting the new year with a new career adventure along with hopefully a new relationship with the man she loved.

All day, she'd been dying to call Chase to share with him her news, but she wanted to surprise him at the party. Bria had reassured he would be there for he'd RSVP'd without a plus one which was a sigh of relief for Brooklyn. The thought of him possibly having a date churned her stomach into knots, but she couldn't be upset if he had another lady on his arm because she was the one who suggested to end things. However, she realized her mistake as soon as he left St. Simons and now she intended to get her man back.

Rustling in her purse, she pulled out her compact mirror and glanced at herself one more time. Bria's glam squad had styled Brooklyn's hair in a curly updo with minimal make up since it wasn't something she wore on an everyday basis. Hot pink lipstick painted her mouth, and there was a light dusting of blush on her cheeks over the foundation that matched her deep caramel skin flawlessly. The emerald earrings that were once in a bracelet owned by her mother were the highlight of her attire.

"All right, girl. I guess you're as ready as you're going to be," Brooklyn said to herself, tossing the compact back in her black, sequined evening clutch that matched her straight, black, sequined dress. She'd thought the slit all the way up to the beginning of her right thigh was a tad too much, but the stylist reassured the dress wasn't going to show anything private. However, it was strapless and her biggest fear wasn't seeing Chase; it was making sure the dress didn't fall down despite the tight way it clung around her body.

Sliding the black, sling-back heels on her manicured feet, she grabbed her purse and matching shawl off the other seat. Wrapping it around her shoulders, Brooklyn knew she should've worn a coat for a few snowflakes had begun to fall as soon as she arrived at the venue. However, she decided to sacrifice warmth for sexy and figured she'd be warm soon enough once she was in the arms of the man she loved.

Moments later, she was greeted at the door by Rasheed's assistant who smiled and nodded as Brooklyn passed through without having to wait in the long line to confirm her name on the guest list. The upbeat music from the jazz band on the stage filled the club, and Brooklyn found herself rocking to the beat and becoming even more excited about seeing Chase.

After checking her shawl at coat check, she spotted Bria who sauntered over in a short, red dress that showcased her long, toned legs. Her back-length, black hair was swept over her right shoulder and a diamond choker graced her neck.

"You look amazing, doll!" Bria complimented, giving Brooklyn a hug. "Our VIP section is upstairs and ... um, your man arrived a moment ago with Addi. They're over by the down stair's bar."

Brooklyn's stomach fluttered uncontrollably at the thought of seeing Chase again. She had her speech all prepared in her head but now it was suddenly a clouded mess as nerves kicked in. *Okay, girl. Be strong. You got this. He loves you and you love him and that's all that matters,* she thought as her feet somehow began to walk on their own toward the bar area as Bria strolled alongside her.

As they approached the vicinity, Brooklyn's heart dropped as she witnessed Chase picking up and twirling a beautiful young woman around in his arms. He proceeded to introduce her to Addison who squealed, clapped, and gave the woman a hug as well.

"Wait." Brooklyn halted, placing a hand on Bria's bare shoulder. "Who's that?" She could barely get the words out as so many different emotions ran rampant through her.

"I have no idea," Bria answered with a wistful sigh. "He didn't have a plus one ..."

"Well. I guess he does."

"Maybe they're just old friends."

"This was a mistake. Clearly he's moved on and I'm too late."

"Don't say that."

"No, it's my fault. I'm the one who suggested we go our separate ways. I mean, he's free to see whoever he wants … Nothing wrong with that." Tears welled in her eyes at the lie she was telling herself, and the last thing she wanted to do was to cry in front of all these people.

"I need some fresh air," Brooklyn said as a heat wave began to rise within her. Wiping her brow, she tried to remain calm and remind herself this was her fault. She couldn't approach him. She couldn't say one damn thing.

"I'll come with you," Bria offered, squeezing her sister-in-law's hand. "Let me just tell Rasheed."

"No. No. You're one of the hosts. I'll be fine."

"You are coming back, right?" Bria asked, her tone filled with concern.

"Of course," Brooklyn answered even though she probably wasn't.

Turning on her heel, she glanced over her shoulder once more at Chase only to catch eyes with his. He smiled and raised his champagne glass to her, but she turned toward the front entrance and fast-walked to it. She vaguely heard her brother call her name through the haze that surrounded her, but she ignored him. Pushing through the crowd of men and women clad in tuxedos and after five attire, she finally landed on the sidewalk as snowflakes touched her skin. In her haste to escape, she'd forgotten to stop by coat check; however, she couldn't go back inside. She placed her arms around herself and trekked briskly toward the next street up.

"Brook," Chase called out, grabbing her upper arm and turning her around to him. "Where are you going?" He took off his trench coat and placed it over her shoulders. "And without a coat? This isn't St. Simons."

"Just g-going f-for a w-walk," she stammered, placing her arms inside the coat with his help. It was warm from his body heat and smelled just like him.

"In the snow wearing a strapless dress. It's hella sexy …" His eyes roamed over it, landing on the side slit before he buttoned the coat up. "I can't have you sick."

"I know how to take care of myself," she said with a confidence that she was glad escaped from her. He couldn't know she was one second away from crying.

"I know. When did you arrive to town?" he asked as if he was baiting her.

Tilting her head, she glared up at him. "I flew in yesterday." *Why does he sound upset? He's the one with the date.*

"Mmm … I see," he said with a nod. Shifting on his feet, he stuffed his hands into his tuxedo pants. "How long are you staying?"

"Not sure."

"The snow is starting to come down faster. Let's head back inside. Its freezing."

"You go ahead. You shouldn't leave your date this long."

"Date?" he asked as his forehead lines scrunched together. "What date?"

"Boy, please. I saw you picking up and twirling around some woman at the bar."

He laughed. Loud. Pulling her toward him, he engulfed her in his embrace. "Jealous?" he questioned, raising a cocky smize up his jaw.

Taken aback, she tried to squirm out of his arms, but he held her still against him. "Jealous? No." *More like ticked at myself for leaving you,* she thought.

"So you stormed out when you saw me with another woman," he stated, wearing the same arrogant grin.

"You can do whatever you want to do. We're not together."

"I know, you've made it clear."

Candace Shaw

"Right, and you have a date waiting for you," she quipped, trying once more to leave his hold, but instead he squeezed her tighter. "Let me go."

"Brooklyn, she's not my date. She's my cousin, Giselle Arrington."

"Who?" she asked, swishing her lips to the side in disbelief. "I know all the Arringtons. Bria said she didn't know who she was."

"She's my late Uncle Sean's daughter. Zoe hired a private investigator to find out if our uncle had any children, and he found Giselle. We invited her to come down from Connecticut for the party to meet the Arrington crew as a surprise to everyone."

"Oh ... so ... wow. I wasn't aware. I'm so sorry for jumping to conclusions."

"Well, maybe if you'd call a brother to let him know you were in Memphis ..."

"Chase, I wanted to surprise you, and when I saw you with her I guess I received a surprise of my own."

"I understand. N-Now can we p-please ... continue this c-conversation inside?" he asked while his teeth chattered as he turned them toward the club. "I have something to tell you."

"Yes, but not here," she replied looping her arm with his. "I want to show you something, first. It's just the next block over on Main Street, and I promise it has heat," she said with reassurance.

A few short moments later, they landed in front of the studio she'd toured earlier. Opening her clutch, she grabbed her keys and proceeded to unlock one of the double glass doors.

"You have the keys to this vacant building?"

"Of course." Opening the door, she flicked up the switch by the entrance. The recess lights brightened the area. Turning off the alarm next to the light switch, she motioned for him to enter the huge, empty industrial

172

space. "I own it," she said in a sing-song voice and a shimmy of the shoulders. "It's all mine."

A wide smile moved across his face slowly. "Really?"

"Yep, bought it today ... well, waiting for the money transfer to clear because of the holiday. The previous owner is a friend of mine who moved to Atlanta recently so she had the real estate agent hand me the keys. Rasheed vouched for me. It needs some renovations, but I hope to have everything up and running by the summer."

"Wait, soooo you're moving back to Memphis?"

"Yes, eventually after I tie up some things on St. Simons. I'll be back and forth with overseeing the renovations. That was my surprise. I'm opening my own photography studio and ..." She paused, as he stepped into her personal space and grabbed her hands.

"Marrying me," Chase finished, pulling her toward him and kissing her tenderly on the lips. He slid a little, black box out of his tuxedo jacket and opened it to display a three-carat, emerald-cut diamond engagement ring.

"Oh my goodness, Chase!" she gasped as she eyed the beautiful, sparkly ring. "How did you know I was moving back home?"

"I didn't, but I knew you would be present tonight, and I'd decided no matter what, I can't be without you. I love you too much, babe. I was going to move to St. Simons or wherever you want to live. Didn't matter. I can open a satellite office anywhere."

"But, Chase, Memphis is your home. I never expected you to leave here for me. That's why I never suggested it."

"I know, but home is where the heart is and that's wherever you are. I love you, Brooklyn."

"I love you, too, Chase. I have for a very long time. I can't believe you were willing to leave Memphis for me, but you don't have to. I'm coming home."

Kneeling in front of her, he slipped the ring on her left ring finger. "Will you marry me, Brooklyn?"

"Yes," she answered, pulling him back up to her and kissing him. "Yes, Chase, I'd love to marry you."

"You just made me the happiest man alive." He picked her up and twirled her around. Placing her back down, he landed another tantalizing kiss on her lips.

"Now let's go tell everyone the great news!" she exclaimed, pulling him toward the door. "It's almost time for the new year."

"And what better way than to be with you, my love? I can't wait to make you my wife."

"And I can't wait to be Mrs. Chase Arrington!"

The End

About Candace Shaw

Candace Shaw writes romance novels because she believes that happily-ever-after isn't found only in fairy tales. When she's not writing or researching information for a book, you can find Candace in her gardens, shopping, reading or learning how to cook a new dish.

Candace lives in Atlanta, Georgia with her loving husband and is currently working on her next fun, flirty, and sexy romance.

You can contact Candace on her website at www.CandaceShaw.net as well as subscribe to her email list for updates, excerpts, and giveaways.

Books by Candace Shaw
The Arrington Family Series

Cooking up Love
The Game of Seduction
Only One for Me
Prescription for Desire
My Kind of Girl

The Chasing Love Series

Her Perfect Candidate
Journey to Seduction
The Sweetest Kiss
His Loving Caress
A Chase for Christmas

The Precious Moments Series

For the Love of You
When I Fell for You
Then There was You
When I Think of You (TBA)

Arrington Family and Friends Series

A Passionate Night

Free Reads

Simply Amazing (Arrington Family Series)
Only You for Christmas (Chasing Love/Harlequin's website
only)

Made in the USA
Columbia, SC
01 April 2020